A ROYAL BIND

SUI LYNN

Dreamspinner Press

Published by
Dreamspinner Press
5032 Capital Circle SW
Ste 2, PMB# 279
Tallahassee, FL 32305-7886
USA
http://www.dreamspinnerpress.com/

Cover Art by L.C. Chase
http://www.lcchase.com

Cover content is being used for illustrative purposes only
and any person depicted on the cover is a model.

ISBN: 978-1-62798-061-6
Digital ISBN: 978-1-62798-062-3

Printed in the United States of America
Second Edition
August 2013

1st Edition published by Silver Publishing, 2012

Praise for Sui Lynn's

A Royal Bind

"…really is an excellent story and lovers of the paranormal genre should give this series a try, but remember that the books have to be read in order so you have to start with the first story."

—Literary Nymphs Reviews

"I was eagerly waiting this second book in the series. I was not disappointed."

—My Earnest Review

"Over all, this was an enjoyable installment in the Changing Moon series and I am looking forward to the next book."

—Hearts on Fire Reviews

To the fans. I can't thank you enough. Your encouragement keeps me writing and the love for the characters... all the characters, the good and bad... sets the stage for each new volume. With your help, there will be many more.

Thank You

PROLOGUE

"IT IS confirmed, Master." The sniveling voice practically whimpered into the phone.

"Did you kill him?" the harsh male voice ground out over the connection.

"No, Master. The assassins are dead. I have confirmation from my contact that the DNA blood tests came back conclusive. Lance Fitz is a pureblood—of the royal line, no less."

"How did this happen! That line has been decimated. They couldn't produce a pure heir even if they tried inbreeding. Hell, they're practically human."

"My contact seems to believe it is a member of the family who is more animal than human and lives as a beast. You know how they go crazy when they lose their mates and revert to an animal and die in the creatures' lifespan. My contact seems to think some member of the family must have remained sane enough to breed, carry and give birth to a child before returning to the wild. Whether the breeding was an accident of two shifters as animals meeting up and having sex or some other oddity of their species that allowed this, we don't know. All we know conclusively is that he is a royal pureblood shifter."

"I want you to get close. Use your contacts, play your part. Get him to trust you. I want this animal brought under control before he can do any more damage. It would be best if you could kill him… quietly… make it look like an accident, if possible. Just make sure he is dead before the shifters realize who he is. Once the royal family and the shifter nation as a whole discover what they have, he'll become a martyr and war will begin again. With our numbers as they are, we will lose. Even against these worthless half-breeds."

"I won't fail you. I'll—"

"You will do as you are told! I'll make the arrangements. You just get close to him, get him to trust you."

"Yes, Master," the voice whimpered, then the connection went dead.

CHAPTER 1

I SAT in the late-afternoon sun up to my elbows in clay. Gwen had told the twins the last time they'd stopped into the Pottery Hut that my stoneware had been selling almost as quickly as she could put it in the window. She only had a couple pieces left and had asked that I make more. I'd never had my work requested before, so there I sat, red clay piled before me, kneading it to the proper consistency. Andrew had gone down to the ranch; he had chores to catch up on. I stared absently at the clay, lost in my thoughts….

TWO weeks…. It's been two weeks since Andrew claimed me… mated with me. Before that, saying my world felt like it was falling apart really would have been an understatement. Everything seemed to be happening so fast I couldn't catch my breath, but we are one now and it's been bliss. The man loves me and I, having grown up not knowing what it was to be loved, am reminded by his constant presence in my mind how much he cares.

You know that old saying life is crazier than fiction? They must have been talking about me. If my life were fiction, it'd be… well, I suppose it'd be on the Horror shelf—I am a monster, after all. Top of the food chain. Well, almost. Everybody keeps telling me the vampires are on the top of the food chain and we shifters come in a close second. Personally, I've met a couple vampires. Granted, they were drones and not born vampires, but still, I'm pretty sure they aren't above me on any food chain when it comes to monsterliness. *I know that's not a word, but you know what I mean. There's no way on this earth a drone could beat me in a fight. In fact, I've already killed two of them, and they were warriors. I'm assuming that born vampires are much stronger because Dr. Tim—who I really like, by the way, and hope to never fight—is also no match for my wolf, despite his hundreds of years of life.*

I guess I should be grateful. If you ignore the insanity that brought me to this point and what that might mean for the future, things are pretty good, though I can't decide if I'm in the eye of the hurricane or if it's just the lull before the storm. If we discount my own feelings at having learned of a whole world I never dreamed was real, and my personal issues as to how I got there as being insignificant to the big picture, then I would guess it's the lull before the storm.

As unbelievable as becoming a shape-shifter once felt, I've become accustomed to my animal spirit's voice. I call him my wolf, though it's much more than just one animal. I'm capable of becoming many different animals. The wolf was the first, then the black falcon. The animal spirit is one and many creatures at the same time. They are all the beast within.

Dr. Tim Carlson, my family's—yes, I'm thinking of Andrew's family as my own, isn't that a shocker—doctor seems to have confirmed my status as the one and only living pureblood shifter. And as if that wasn't enough, my bloodline is not only

4

pure, but also royal. Somewhere, Fate has to be just rolling on the floor, laughing her ass off. I mean, really, a street brat nobody wanted and now I'm royalty—me, of all people. Yeah, it's a mind fuck. I'm still getting used to it.

WITH a deep breath, I reached down into the bowl beside me, grabbed the cup and scooped up some water to add to my clay, then dropped the cup back into the basin of water. The consistency still wasn't right. I stared at the pile of earth before me, unable to shake the musings that fluttered about my mind....

IT SEEMS as if I come by this crazy life naturally. My mother was seriously messed up, and I think she must still be, if I understand what everyone's telling me. Somewhere out there in the wild, among the real animals, my parents are alive and living as beasts. Mommy dearest couldn't live with her broken heart after her vampire lover died. But because her mate was a vampire and not another shifter, she couldn't bond fully with him and therefore wasn't allowed death after a single animal lifetime. I guess even the love of a child wasn't enough for her because she abandoned me like yesterday's trash in a world she had to have known I might not survive. But who knows how much of her mind is still human. She's lived as an animal for more than three hundred years, since the beginning of the war between shifters and vampires. I can't judge her for her love. If I knew my love for Andrew would start a war, would I continue to love him? Without any doubt or hesitation, my answer is yes. Because my love for him isn't really a choice. I just do. Not saying I want to start wars or anything, but I refuse to give him up for any reason. I guess that makes me selfish, but I won't apologize for having love in my life. After growing up the way I did, without so much as a caring parent, I think I deserve whatever love I can find, and Andrew is one of a kind and he's all mine.

Grant me the serenity to accept the things I cannot change, the courage to change the things I can, and the wisdom to know the difference. I recited the mantra to myself that's become a truism in my life and asked myself, what can I possibly change? I know I can't change who my biological parents are, so I need to come to terms with this royal pureblood thing. I can't control others' reactions to who or what I am, but I don't want some stupid title to come back and bite me in the ass. Ultimately, the only thing I can control is myself. Beyond that, I might be able to influence those around me, hopefully in a positive manner. Even a royal pureblood only has so much power in a world where vampires rule, and one of those vampires holds Andrew's life in his hands—Stephon.

LOST in the past, I had no idea how long I'd stared at the drying clay. The fact the outer edges were beginning to crust told me I'd been walking through my thoughts for quite some time. I looked up and saw Andrew coming toward me from across the meadow, the warm fall sun making his golden skin glow. He wore a cowboy hat, the rim casting a shadow over his eyes. With his powerful arms bare, the sleeveless western shirt only half-buttoned, and worn dusty blue jeans riding low on his hips, hugging his body in all the right places, the man was a vision.

He must have finished his chores at the ranch, and here I was still sitting with the same pile of clay I'd had when he left a couple hours ago. I looked about me and shook my head at how little I'd accomplished. The sun was already setting low over the horizon, and it was apparent the day had slipped away from me. I hoped he'd gotten more done than I had.

Missed you, leannan. His voice, soft as velvet, was like a caress as I heard it in my mind. He always called me that. Leannan—beloved.

The sound of his voice, even if just in my mind, settled my restless thoughts. Andrew was ruggedly handsome. His high cheekbones and straight nose hinted at some Native American blood, but the way he spoke, with just a touch of a Scottish lilt, and those deep-blue eyes indicated he descended from the Emerald Isle. He came around the table and I found myself surrounded by him. Just being there in his arms calmed me. I couldn't let anyone hurt him, but since there was no way to prevent the future consequences of my past actions, we'd just have to ride things out and hope for the best.

Not going to happen. I'm not going anywhere and we are united. Not even Stephon can change that now. Andrew shored up my wavering self-confidence. When he was with me I had no doubts; it was when I was alone that doubts about my survival in this new world tended to get to me.

I felt a mental zing shoot through Andrew's mind. It had been happening more often than I liked. *This is our time. There is time for us to deal with him later. It isn't a problem right now, and I want our time to be ours.* Andrew's voice eased the raw edge developing in my mind. I knew from the memories Andrew had passed to me in our bonding that the mental sting was Stephon calling. And the more Andrew ignored him, the more persistent the vampire would become in his mental demands— and the more painful the contact.

"He's not going away." I leaned back against Andrew's chest.

"No. I'm afraid he's as permanent a fixture in my life as my parents are. The only difference is Mom picks up the phone when she wants to talk to me, and Stephon… well, he reaches out and touches my mind." Andrew kissed the top of my head.

"I hate it. Nobody should touch you—any part of you—but me!" My wolf growled at the irritation caused by Stephon's presence in our lives. I was growing to hate the vampire and the hold he had on my mate more and more each day.

"I know, but he has always had a hold of a corner of my mind. It's just the way things are. Maybe if we can convince Stephon to release me, then who knows… you might end up being the only one in my mind. To be honest, I don't even know if the mental bond is possible to break. It's been there since shortly after my birth."

"I don't have to like it, though. It pisses my wolf off, and I guess I've gotten possessive. You belong to me and I belong to you. No one else should have a part of you." My wolf snarled, and I held him back from mentally sniffing around in Andrew's mind. He wanted to hunt down the bond between Andrew and the vampire and shred it. I was afraid of what that might do to Andrew, so I forced the wolf to wait. Thoughts of Stephon always had me thinking about the warrior drones that had attacked us a couple of months ago, when Andrew had returned from his trip to see his benefactor. To me, the two were connected. It seemed to be too much of a coincidence that we were attacked so soon after his return, but Andrew insisted Stephon wasn't capable of hurting his beneficiaries. I tried not to let my suspicions run away with me, for Andrew's sake. If our attacker wasn't Stephon, then who else could know and want me dead?

"Come on, let's get you cleaned up. We have company coming." Andrew gave me a squeeze before releasing me.

"Are we even remotely ready for this?" I whispered with a slight shake of my head.

"We might not be ready, but we're strong. You can't anticipate everything. Ultimately, we don't know how people are going to react, but together we can face anything. And you know

I'll never leave you." Andrew took my hand and tugged me up onto my feet.

"Okay."

Andrew glanced down at the red clay that now clung to his arms and hands. "I think we both need to get cleaned up." Sighing, I followed him into the cottage.

I let Andrew lead me through the house to the bathroom. I stared as he stripped out of his clothes and stepped into the shower. My own actions seemed sluggish by comparison, as if the thoughts weighing on my mind slowed my limbs as well, but I did eventually make it, and stepped into the hot spray. I just wished I could focus my attention on the beautiful golden-skinned god before me, but knowing someone wanted you dead was a real buzzkill. Andrew pulled me in front of him and began to wash the red clay from my hands and arms, pressing himself against my back. By the time he dragged his hands across my chest, the combination of the slick soap and hot water, along with Andrew's touch and scent, had the blood pooling in my groin. Any thought not centered on him vanished from my mind.

Andrew rubbed his hand across my stomach, down to my groin, and took hold of the base of my cock. I couldn't have kept the groan from escaping my lips if I'd wanted to. Andrew ran his hands up my sides to my arms, then guided them up and around his neck.

Hold on to me, his mental voice whispered in my mind. I obeyed, cradling the back of his neck with one hand while burying the fingers of the other in his thick hair. My knees felt like rubber as he stroked back down over my arms to my pecs, where he stopped to tease my nipples. I widened my stance, allowing his cock to slip between my thighs. Andrew groaned, my balls bumping him as he ground himself against my ass.

"Andrew," I gasped, my breath catching with each twist of my nips. His touch was like an electrical current, lighting up my

9

body. His desire burned through our bond, tingling through his fingers as he caressed my slick skin. I turned my head to the side and stretched for his kiss. He didn't disappoint, lightly gliding his lips across mine, brushing gently back and forth. I slipped my tongue past his lips and tasted him—so masculine, with a touch of coffee he must have had while at the ranch—tantalizing my taste buds. Taking my mouth, he plundered it, sinking his tongue deep, demanding my response.

A growl rumbled inside him. The vibrations from his chest tingled across my back, making me arch into him, pushing my hips back against his. He shifted his hold, putting one arm across my chest, the hairs on his forearm brushing against the sensitized flesh of my nipples as he slid his other hand along my abdomen. When he reached the short curls on my groin, he moved his fingers in slow circles amongst the hairs, teasing and enticing me. His touch was so gentle, yet it held such passion, driving all thoughts from my mind, along with the air from my lungs.

"An-Andrew!" I cried out as he released my lips and nipped at my jaw. I instinctively tilted my head to the side, giving him more room. I loved the feeling of his lips on my neck.

"You're so strong." Andrew bit down on my neck, not breaking the skin, but hard enough for me to feel the burn as he released and licked at the abused flesh. "Thinking… you're always thinking. That brain of yours only slows down when I've got you like this. You work yourself into circles, vacillating between the things you don't know and the things you fear." The pinch of pain behind my ear and the tight grip on my erection made me dig my fingernails into his skin. I thrust my hips, pushing my cock forward into his grip, while he rubbed his own between my asscheeks.

"Please Andrew… I need…," I begged incoherently as I humped at his fist.

"I know what you're thinking. Your wolf's getting all protective of me... of our family." My knees quaked. I could hardly stand as my balls began to tighten and draw up. Andrew felt it too. He took a firm grip at the base of my cock and squeezed, not letting me come.

"Ahhh—" I screamed, denied my release.

"Not yet. I'm not finished with you," he whispered, and then he nibbled on my ear. My arms quaked as shivers of my denied release flowed through my body. "You don't seem to understand love. You've been alone so long, I guess it makes sense that love would be a mystery to you. But I'm going to love on you until you get it."

As the trembling from my denied orgasm slowed to a simmer, Andrew began to stroke my erection again. He slid his tight fist down the length then slowly back up to circle the glans, then fisted the head with a twist of his rough callused hand. I swore I could feel each groove and line on his work-hardened skin as he stoked the fires of my passion. "We are one. That means whatever's coming, it isn't just you who has to face it. You. Are. *Not.* Alone." He punctuated each word with a tug on my shaft and a nip to my neck that I was sure would bring up a bruise.

"Andrew...," I panted, my lust rising, the thrust of my hips becoming erratic.

"Say it, leannan. I need to know you understand."

"Say...." I shook my head, understanding coming slowly through the haze of need. He expected an answer from my lust-fuzzed brain.

"Lance, lean on me. Together we're strong and we can be anything. You just have to let me help. Stop trying to take on the world alone."

"God, Andrew… I can't think when you're…." His attentions made me feel like my body was turning into Jell-O. I leaned back into his arms, knowing he wouldn't let me fall. My brain was mush, but I could feel his underlying need.

"That's it. Trust me. I'll always be here to catch you." Andrew growled his approval as my body automatically understood and gave my mate what he needed. I'd forgotten—he was the alpha, my big strong man who needed to take care of me just as much as I wanted to take care of him.

"Please, Andrew…," I gasped. How stupid to be working on plans to keep us alive, but not tell him. Of course he knew what I'd been doing because of our mental connection. He could hear me mulling over the issues and feel my self-doubt.

"You need to understand, Lance. It isn't just you anymore. We're in this together, and you need to talk to me."

"Yes. I trust you." My words, barely audible, seemed to ease the frustration I could feel coming off him in waves. "Love you. Need only you."

He began to jack me in earnest, playing with my balls as he did. I rocked my head from side to side on his shoulder, trying to hold off my orgasm, knowing I needed to wait for him to let me come. Andrew required my obedience, my submission, and I gave it willingly… gratefully. I craved his control, his power over me. It centered me as nothing else could. I wanted him to make the decisions—not because I couldn't, or was afraid to—but because some part of me desired to be cared for, coddled, even. Andrew wanted to take care of me, and I needed to let him do it.

"Come now," Andrew growled, as he sank his teeth into the flesh of my shoulder.

"Andrew," I screamed as the overwhelming bliss of my orgasm rocked my body and cum shot over his hand and onto the shower wall. Andrew howled. He released my shoulder and pulled back just a little, allowing his hot spunk to cover my back. His breath sent aftershocks through my body as he milked every drop from my softening cock. Never once did his hold on me waver, nor was I afraid that passion would knock him off his feet. He was my rock, steady and sure. I understood.

I love you so much. Even my mental voice sounded soft and sated. I felt Andrew's deep chuckle against my back in the very core of my body.

You are my life. So share it with me. He kissed my temple and with his free hand, he grabbed the body wash from a shelf in the shower. I turned in his arms as a soapy cloth slid along my skin, removing the remnants of our loving. By the time my muscles were able to obey my commands again, Andrew was gently leading me from the shower and wrapping a towel around me. He vigorously rubbed the moisture from my body before seeing to his own needs.

"Tim called while I was at the ranch. He's gathered the vassals, and they're coming to meet you."

"Great… just what I need—more vampires." I couldn't prevent the troubled sigh that escaped me.

"I won't let anything happen to you. Tim says he trusts these two, and it's important for us to have some support from the vampires. Have a little faith." Andrew handed me a comb before heading to the bedroom for some clothes.

He was right. We needed the vampires. The more support we could gather, the better. But faith in others was hard for me to give, even with Andrew guiding the way. After a lifetime of rejection and abandonment, trust wasn't handed out lightly.

CHAPTER 2

I COULD hear voices. While I had finished cleaning up, Tim and his friends must have arrived. Deciding to dress casual, I grabbed a pair of jeans and a green T-shirt. I didn't care about the whole royalty thing, and I refused to be something I wasn't. It would be best if they realized right up front I was no prince. Once I was ready, I opened the bedroom door and stepped out into the kitchen.

Andrew's eyes lit up as I entered the room, and he extended a hand toward me. I took it and moved to take my place beside him, leaning against his side. Tim stood by the door, and he smiled at us while two people I'd never seen before waited behind him in the open doorway. Looking at Andrew, Tim frowned slightly and then nodded as if he'd made a discovery.

"Good evening!" he greeted us with a smile.

"Hi, Tim." I motioned for him to come in. Upon entering, he came straight to both of us and wrapped an arm around each of our shoulders, hugging us.

With his head between ours, he whispered, "It's so good to see you've settled your differences. I'm so happy for you.

Congratulations." I felt his little squeeze on my shoulder. He released us and stepped back, giving us a grin, then turned to the people who remained waiting at the door.

"Lance, Andrew, these are a couple of old friends I'd like to introduce you to. They were with me all those years ago. We're all children of Lord Basil, drones who were once in service to Lord Nathaniel, the vampire your mother chose as her mate. We all swore to serve her as vassals."

"Welcome." Andrew smiled, but pulled me slightly behind him in a display of protective instinct. The vampires nodded to us as Tim closed the door behind them.

"Won't you have a seat?" I motioned to the large oak kitchen table.

Andrew pulled my chair closer to his so our thighs were touching under the table, and laced our fingers together as we held hands. Taking a deep breath, I prepared for the worst and tried to hold on to the fact that regardless of whether Tim's friends accepted me or not, Andrew always would.

I watched as they all took their seats. Tim's friends were very different from him. Tim looked every bit the small-town doctor in his brown trousers, white button-down shirt, simple tie, and matching brown jacket. He reminded me of Doctor Who—the tenth one, not the eleventh.

The two vampires he had brought with him were very much his opposite. The woman looked lethal, the ultimate female warrior: tall and slim, a predator in grace and motion, one that promised silent death when crossed. Like Tim, she had a chalky white complexion and black eyes, but that was where the similarity ended. She wore black leather pants tucked into thigh-high leather boots, and a studded black-leather bra with an open, white button-down shirt over the top. She carried a whip on her hip, as well as an assortment of sheathed throwing knives attached to a belt around her waist. Her sleek, shoulder-length black hair had vivid red tips and fell across one eye.

The other vampire, a male, truly stood at the opposite end of the spectrum from the woman. He wore black dress slacks, leather loafers, and a white button-down shirt with a short-sleeved V-neck argyle sweater vest over it. A black silk cravat with a diamond pin adorned his throat. A black sports coat was draped over his arm. His black hair, sleek and glossy—a pompadour, complete with ducktail—reminded me of John Travolta's appearance in *Grease*. Where Travolta pulled it off and was hot, this guy just screamed "loser geek." The only things missing were a pocket protector, horn-rimmed glasses, and an overbite, although I was sure he could flash a pair of wicked fangs if he so chose. The only similarities among the three were their black eyes and chalky white skin.

"This is my older kinswoman, Charlie, and Brad, a younger kinsman." Tim indicated the woman on his right and then the man on his left as they took their seats.

Charlie openly stared at me. "His resemblance to his parents is remarkable."

"You said he has unprecedented abilities?" Brad looked toward Tim for confirmation.

"Yes. Lance has only been transforming for a little over six months, and he's mastered two forms—a black falcon and a brown wolf."

"Mmm, yes. Considering his parentage, that'd be very likely. Does he know where his parents are?" asked Charlie. They continued their conversation as if we weren't even there; I was merely a specimen on display.

"No. He's been in human care since infancy." Tim shook his head, as if my upbringing troubled him greatly.

"I'm sitting right here, you can ask *me*, you know," I grumbled, but Tim just grinned and the conversation among the three flowed on around me.

"How unfortunate. If his parents could be found.... Well, then there'd be other complications." Brad pursed his lips thoughtfully, as he seemed to consider the possible consequences of my parents' arrival.

"I'm sure the genetic test results are flawless, Tim," said Charlie. "He even smells like his mother. There's no doubt in my mind at all as to who he is. They're both there. I can see them in his person."

Tim nodded. "Yes, I figured you of all of us would be the easiest to convince, Charlie. You spent the most time with Sasha. If I could see the resemblance, I knew you would as well."

"I saw Sasha last, before she and her protector, Henry Fitz, disappeared into the woods." Charlie shook her head. "What a waste. I don't need to discuss this any further, Tim." She turned to me and looked me in the eyes, truly acknowledging me for the first time. "I'm your vassal, my prince. If you have need of me, all you need do is call."

"Ah.... Th-thank you?" I stuttered, my reply coming out more as a question than a statement of gratitude.

Charlie smiled, and it was chilling to behold. "I am a warrior. I used to be part of your mother's security, assigned to her by my former lord, the born vampire Lord Nathaniel." She handed Andrew a slip of paper with a phone number on it. "If either of you ever have need of me, just call and I'll come immediately." Charlie briefly bowed her head and closed her eyes as she made her vow.

"Thank you." Andrew returned her bow.

"I think we need to contact Father." Brad frowned at Charlie. "Consult him before we start swearing oaths."

"Why? Father was always in favor of Lord Nathaniel and Lady Sasha's relationship. He even supported them when Prince Henry swore to be her protector before the war. I can't see him turning his back on her son and his mate." Charlie narrowed her eyes and put her shoulders back, as if her honor had been affronted.

"You can't say that for sure. His mother cost Father his only born son. Neither of you have been home in a very long time. How can you say what his reaction will be?" Brad fumed.

"The oaths were said more than three hundred years ago. Father would expect us to uphold our honor. This is just an affirmation. My oath to Lady Sasha would automatically include any progeny, as does yours." Charlie hissed, the tip of a fang appearing over her bottom lip.

"My father would never do anything to sully his son's memory, including turning away or attempting to harm the child of one he considered his daughter. How can you think so little of him?" Tim growled at Brad. "You live in his house, work for him in his businesses, and still you judge him so poorly?"

"I'm not saying you aren't right. I'm just saying we should contact him first," Brad insisted, crossing his arms over his chest.

Charlie rolled her eyes and turned back to me. Obviously done with Brad's dissension, she changed the subject. "Tim said there was an attack. That two drones tried to kill you?"

"Yes. A couple weeks ago. We were returning home and met my brothers and a cousin just beyond the tree line, entering the meadow. We were about to go hunting when the drones approached from the northern edge of the tree line." Andrew squeezed my hand and continued. "They were decked out in full battle gear and body armor. I'd never seen anything like Lance, though. The drones were trained warriors, but fairly young by your standards, I think. If it'd been just us without Lance, it would've been a pretty even fight, but Lance cut them down like they were merely a nuisance."

"A drone rarely stood a chance against a pureblood shifter, and today's warriors aren't trained like we were in the old days on how to fight against a pure shifter." Charlie seemed thoughtful.

"You've always been fast, Lance. But that night, you moved like lightning." Andrew reached over and kissed me gently on the lips. "You were truly magnificent to see."

"Be that as it may, enough drones can take down a pureblood," Brad grumped. He stared at the ceiling, as if the act of looking me in the eyes would dirty him. I was beginning to strongly dislike Brad.

"He's an ass, but he's right," Charlie remarked as she gave Brad a smack on the back of the head. "I'm going to start calling together a guard for you. I'll let you know when we arrive. This is a good location. It's remote and easily defended. There's only one way in or out. And the ranch practically stands guard over the entrance to your driveway. Just be aware that the more you make yourself known, the more threats there will be to your life."

"I agree. Do you have anyone particular in mind for this guard?" Tim scowled at Brad and sighed in frustration.

"I do. I need to make a few phone calls and see who's available. It'll take a few days." Charlie looked down at her hands in concentration. "I'm pretty sure I can draw together five or six. That'll be a good group to start. I'm sure there'll be more, especially once Father gets involved."

"You really think I need to get another born vampire involved in this? I mean, isn't having to deal with Stephon enough?" I asked the three vampires.

I keep telling you, Stephon is not the bad guy here, Andrew grumbled in my mind. Maybe I was being stubborn about the whole Stephon thing, but until he freed my man, my opinion of him would remain unchanged. Even though Andrew knew my feelings on the subject, I wouldn't argue about it with him, as it was pointless to do so. For now, we remained at an impasse.

"You really think a guard is necessary? I mean, won't that just draw more attention to him? Make him appear militant?" Brad's pessimism was beginning to grate, and it was all I could do to keep from snarling.

"Militant? Really? I'm just trying to not get killed here." I practically had to close my eyes to keep them from rolling up into my skull in a show of extreme frustration.

"It is necessary. Besides, with the right people, nobody will know the guard's here," Charlie argued.

"Fine, but I'm not going to be the one to tell Father. This is your secret, Tim. You tell him."

"I still think you're making too much of this, Brad. Father's going to be overjoyed and he'll probably feel badly that he didn't know about Lance when he was living amongst the humans." Tim put a reassuring hand on Brad's shoulder. "Brother, our father will treat Lance like a grandchild."

"You really think he'll be happy to meet me?" I couldn't help but ask. Tim was acting as if this vampire would think of me as a long-lost loved one. With all the rejection I'd gotten over the years, I'd long ago given up on being part of a family. Andrew's family had become the exception. They cared about me and wanted me because Andrew loved me. I wasn't sure I wanted to put myself out there again. When I was in the foster program, even though each new family had brought a possibility for acceptance and love, I'd always been rejected. Of course I understood why now—I wasn't human, and even though I was unaware, human instinct prevailed. I was a predator among sheep. This pureblood vampire, the father of my mother's mate, was the closest thing to my own family I'd probably ever get. Could I take the chance? Could I put my feelings out there even with the possibility of being rejected yet again? And by a born vampire no less?

"I'm more than sure. But if you prefer, I'll wait until you have your business settled with Stephon before setting up a meeting. Truthfully, Lord Basil might be able to influence Stephon. Maybe he can even encourage him to release Andrew." Tim met Charlie's eyes, and she nodded her agreement.

"Are they friends?" I had to know.

"Umm... no. They don't exactly run in the same circles." Andrew practically flinched, but I wasn't sure why. Andrew was uncomfortable and seemed almost embarrassed for Stephon.

"Stephon runs with a wilder crowd than Lord Basil." Charlie chuckled. "In the vampire world, Stephon's a party boy and Lord Basil is a member of the ruling council. The two would be unlikely to spend much time together or have much in common."

"Stephon's a party boy? You made him out to sound like a scholar." I frowned at Andrew.

"Well, yeah, I mean, the man is hundreds of years old. Going to university was more or less for me. He'd been through it many times before. He spent most of his time partying like a frat boy."

"My opinion of him just keeps getting better and better." I barely kept the disgust from my voice. That was something I would love to be able to do—attend school and learn art, literature... any number of subjects, really. And vamp boy partied his way through university?

"Stephon is, by far, one of the better benefactors the shifter community has. He actively works to improve the conditions for his charges. There are some who try just as hard to prevent shifters from improving their lot in life." Even Charlie was backing my nemesis now. I just sighed and tried to move on.

"Okay, so Charlie's going to get a few bodyguards together. Tim's going to tell Lord Basil about me. Is there anything else?" The whole discussion was becoming a bit much, and my ability to accept my part in this new world was very limited at the moment.

They're doing their best. I know you're trying. After they leave, we'll go hunting and you can run off some of your frustration. Andrew, ever my rock, calmed my growing agitation with a simple thought. I'd love to run and hunt, to free my wolf and not have to think about any of this for a while.

"There's something still bothering you. Something more than just what we've discussed," Tim remarked—ever the observant doctor. In the short time he'd come to know me, the man had already picked up on the fact that my outbursts of frustration or temper were usually a defense mechanism for when something was eating at me.

"Tim, are you mentally linked as well?" I blurted out. The mental bond between Stephon and Andrew was the one thing that really irked my wolf. I needed to know more about it.

"What do you mean mentally linked… you mean to each other?" Tim looked to Charlie; they both seemed confused by what I'd said.

"No." I almost regretted opening my mouth now, but I needed answers.

They might have an understanding of this bond Stephon and I share, that even I don't know about. But remember, they're just drones, so they may not be totally aware of the link formed between shifter charges and their vampire benefactor. Andrew's voice was all the encouragement I needed to ask my questions.

"Andrew is mentally connected to Stephon, has been since he was a baby and became Stephon's responsibility. I'm wondering if you, as drones, are connected to a born vampire as well."

"Ah...." Tim nodded his understanding. "A drone, when first created, is mentally tethered to his creator. Lord Basil saved my life. If he hadn't turned me, I would've died. But a newborn drone is very violent, and we have a lot of trouble controlling our base instincts. There are only two things that guide a newborn drone—blood and sex. The need for both overwhelms us completely. Without being tethered to our creator, we'd be practically mindless for at least the first year or two, possibly longer, if allowed to run amok. So we're mentally tied to our creator, who then has a measure of control over us. This mental connection continues until the creator chooses to relinquish it, usually after the drone has lived thirty or forty years and shown they can be trusted to control themselves amongst humans." Tim looked to Charlie.

"When our father felt we'd grown and proven ourselves to be 'adult' vampires, able to make our own decisions, a celebration was held. A kind of a coming-of-age thing. We were released from his control and allowed to go out and fend for ourselves. Unlike many, Lord Basil has always wanted his children near him. We are independent of him and he allows us to make our own decisions, but he likes to be a part of our lives." Charlie's smile was so soft and tender, filled with such love for her creator, her father... it made the hard deadly warrior momentarily fade into the countenance of a lovingly gentle daughter. The look didn't last long.

"So the tether can be removed, if not broken?" Andrew asked.

"Well, yes. Both, in fact. There are times when a creator and drone disagree. If the drone has become strong enough, he can break away from his creator, snapping the mental connection. Depending on the age and maturity of the drone, sometimes creator and drone just go their separate ways. Other times the creator will hunt down and eliminate his creation for his defiance. The consequences of breaking the connection really depend on the born vampire." Tim shrugged.

"What about Andrew's connection?" Andrew stroked my thigh under the table, trying to soothe away the tension he felt building in me.

"It depends on Andrew. If he's strong enough to break away from Stephon's mental connection, then I don't see why he couldn't." Tim stared into Andrew's eyes, then smiled. "Since your mating, you've become much stronger, Andrew. The power radiating from you is pretty much equal to Lance's. I believe it's as I suspected—once the two of you became bound to each other, your powers also linked and balanced out, making you equals. In essence, Andrew is now as much of a pureblood as Lance is."

"So we should be able to break away without any repercussions, at least as far as anyone getting hurt?"

"I don't see why not. Stephon will probably be a bit put out, but I wouldn't expect there to be any actual physical issues."

I couldn't help the gratified chuckle that escaped me. Stephon was about to get to see just how annoyed my wolf was. If there was no real possibility of repercussion, then there was no reason not to hunt the bond in Andrew's mind and shred the connection. *Stephon can learn to use a phone, instead of buzzing my mate's mind whenever he wants.* "Thanks, Tim. You've definitely given me a goal to achieve."

"Good. We need to make sure you keep your independence. I think it would be best to change Andrew's social status as a beneficiary and gain his freedom as quickly as possible," Charlie said. "I believe the severing of the mental tether would be a good first step to proving you are indeed capable of independence. In our society, it would be how a drone would prove his ability to act independently of our parent." She nodded, then grinned a toothy and rather evil smile. "Besides, if you succeed, the backlash from the bond being severed abruptly will most likely give Stephon a headache…. Bonus."

"You're not fond of Stephon?" I asked. Charlie was beginning to grow on me.

"I'll only say there's no love lost between us." Charlie rose from her chair. "He's a bit frivolous and self-absorbed for my taste." Tim and Brad stood, moving to join her. "I think we've accomplished everything we needed to, gentlemen. Andrew, Lance, I'll contact you as soon as I have your guard together. In the meantime, be careful to whom you make your presence known. And if you even *think* something feels out of the ordinary, call me. I'll return as soon as I can."

"Before we leave, I'll stop by the ranch and speak to your folks about the added security. If you've any questions, please call me," Tim said. "Let me know when you're ready to confront Stephon regarding your social status as a beneficiary. I'll see to it you're adequately escorted in the event he decides against freeing you. I might be able to buy you some time, but it won't be much. I don't know how long the royals will wait before contacting you, either. In any case, Stephon will need to be notified before you formally have an audience with the royals." His comments were mostly directed to Andrew as I had become rather preoccupied with thoughts of how to sever Stephon's mental link. I stood along with everyone else and saw our friends—and Brad—out.

"Prince Lance, I am forever your vassal." Tim smiled at me and bowed.

"I am forever your vassal, Prince Lance, and at your service," Charlie said, also bowing.

"At your service, my prince." Brad bowed just as the others had, but the look in his eyes and his frown conveyed his objections, even as he pledged his service.

"Until you call on us," Tim said in parting. With that, the three vampires were out the door and to the car almost faster than I could see them go. The car started and they took off down the road.

CHAPTER 3

I AWOKE to sunlight streaming in through our bedroom window. We still needed to get some damn curtains; waking up with the sun in my eyes was getting old. Andrew lay wrapped around me, while my head lay pillowed against his chest. The vibrations of his gentle snoring rumbled in my ear. My stomach let loose an answering growl. Food was a definite priority.

Andrew looked so serene as he slept. The past week had been good for both of us; we'd needed the recuperation time. Much of the gauntness and exhaustion from our prolonged separation and his visit with Stephon had vanished. He'd gained a few pounds, the hollow, sunken look around his eyes now a thing of the past.

For a moment, I simply watched him as he slept. My hunger could wait. I couldn't help but grin as his stomach growled noisily. Andrew's eyes fluttered open, perhaps awakened by the sound of his own hunger. With a yawn and stretch, he beamed with happiness as he looked into my eyes.

"Good morning," he mumbled and kissed me on the nose.

"Good morning." As I spoke, I shuddered at the taste of my own breath. I desperately needed to brush my teeth.

His stomach protested its emptiness again, and I couldn't resist the temptation to tease. "Hungry, love?"

My stomach grumbled in reply, and it was his turn to smirk. "Well, at least I'm not the only one." We both laughed. Andrew threw back the covers, and after taking me by the hand, led me from our bed. I stumbled clumsily as my feet hit the floor and I fell heavily against his chest.

"Oomph." He grunted as I knocked the breath from his lungs. His arms were instantly there, preventing me from falling to the floor. I flushed with embarrassment. *Yeah, real predatorial grace I've got; can't even stand up in the morning.*

"How about you go take a shower and I'll start breakfast." Andrew's smile eased my irritation. I couldn't stay grumpy with him around.

"Okay." I leaned in for a quick, closed-mouth kiss, only to pull back as he began teasing and nibbling at my bottom lip. "Umm... bad idea. Really bad morning breath." I covered my mouth with my hand, trying not to cringe. *Need to remember to brush my teeth after hunting.*

Andrew chuckled at my thought. He kissed me on the forehead and gave me a gentle push toward the bathroom. As he made his way to the kitchen, I caught a glimpse of his beautiful bare ass. My wolf urged me to go and watch Andrew cook naked, but my halitosis had me nearly running for the bathroom. I needed to freshen up so I could kiss that luscious man.

After I emerged from my ablutions, I walked through our bedroom and joined him in the main room. I paused in the doorway, taking a moment to just enjoy our home. The cottage, my sanctuary, was small, just big enough for the two of us. The main room was both kitchen and living room in one. I still marveled at the beautiful furnishings Andrew had brought to the cabin, and the forest-green rugs Andrew had purchased. The kitchen table and chairs, carved with wolves in the backrests, still amazed me. He'd taken the run-down shack and created a niche to keep the world away.

Andrew stood in the far corner of the room, bent over, fussing with the stereo. The man had a luscious ass. I itched to give it a squeeze, but if we started then neither of us would be eating anytime soon. I laughed as the downbeat of Huey Lewis and the News's "The Heart of Rock and Roll" blasted throughout the cabin. Sometimes his taste surprised me. I walked into the kitchen and began going through the cupboards, seeing what I could find for—I glanced at the clock—lunch. We'd really slept in; it was later than either of us had realized.

By the time Andrew joined me in the kitchen, I'd decided we'd have to go shopping. "We're going to need to get some supplies. Our cupboard is starting to look a bit on the empty side." I took the last of the steaks from the fridge and the last of the potatoes from a bag in the kitchen cabinet. I used up the last of the onions and green peppers. I found a bag of frozen green beans and asparagus. The meal came together nicely in no time at all. We sat down to eat, enjoying just being together.

After closing my eyes and taking a deep breath, I broached a subject I knew we had to discuss, but I wasn't sure how receptive Andrew would be. I opened my eyes and said, "We need to choose a third form. I don't want to rush into this. I don't want to do anything before we're both ready, but I thought we should at least talk about it."

"I know," Andrew sat back in the chair. "Since we bonded, I can feel your power in me. I think Tim's right. It really feels like I share a portion of your power. We aren't two separate beings anymore, but more one soul and two bodies. The power of both of us combined. I feel like I can do anything you can do." Andrew winked and sipped his coffee.

"Is that a challenge, love?" I teased, licking my lips.

Andrew growled. "A promise... for later."

I practically whimpered as he groped my thigh, brushing his fingers against the bulge in my jeans, but I forced my brain to continue. "I've been considering a couple of different animals, but I'm not sure what would be the most impressive to the vampires and royals. I guess I'm thinking something powerful and unique would be better than ordinary."

"You're right in thinking powerful. In our world, like the animal world, power is everything. Think of the food chain—the most powerful and feared beings at the top are the ones that are messed with the least."

"So bigger and deadlier is better than cute and cuddly?"

"Yeah. When I think of the stories about the ancients, they took many different forms, but none of them could've ever been thought to be ordinary."

"Okay, so what do you think? A big cat, like a tiger, a lion? Or an elephant, maybe?" I watched his face. Over the past couple of weeks, we'd hunted as wolves and flown as falcons, but we hadn't tried anything new despite Tim's encouragement to choose a third form.

"None of the ancients ever chose an herbivore. An elephant would definitely be impressive and a force to be reckoned with. It'd also be a hard shape to demonstrate in an enclosed room, in the middle of a bunch of other shape-shifters and vampires—all predators, by the way. I don't think even an elephant could remain calm." Andrew wrinkled his brow in thought. "You could end up hurting friends as well as enemies in a mad rampage. It'd be unique and impressive, but probably not the best idea."

"Yeah, I see what you mean. Okay, sticking to carnivores, then."

"And some omnivores, like bears. I don't believe there're any amongst the royals who can pull off a predator as massive and powerful as a tiger. I think there's a panther amongst them, and I'm almost sure one of the older women in the family is a lioness. None of them have more than one animal." Andrew locked his gaze onto mine.

"What about bears?"

"The big cats are showier, although bears do have a lot of raw power. Still, I think the idea of a tiger would be better than a bear or any other of the major predators. There aren't many other animals that'd take on a tiger and survive. Besides, I think I'd enjoy being a tiger." He grinned so sincerely that I knew the idea had merit to him. Although the pain involved in choosing yet another animal was daunting to both of us, knowing we'd chosen together put me more at ease.

"Okay. Tiger it is." I chuckled. Having finished our meal, we piled our dirty dishes in the sink. "Have you checked your phone? Has anyone called?"

"I checked, but no one's called. I think they're trying to give us as much alone time as they can before the craziness starts."

"What do you mean 'before the craziness starts'? You mean it hasn't started yet?" I gasped in mock surprise. I didn't want things to get too serious. The day seemed to be ours to while away.

"Come... fly with me." His eyes lit up at the idea. "We have the whole day to ourselves. Let's have some fun on the wing."

"I'd love to." His transformation into the falcon had gotten much smoother and faster with each flight, and now we could both become the falcon as easily as we did our wolves.

31

"Yes, the falcon calls to me." Excitement lit his eyes, as it always did when he thought about the freedom of the skies.

"Okay. Let's go."

He winked and the race was on. He yanked off his T-shirt and started removing his sweatpants and socks, hobbling toward the door in his rush to be the first one free of his clothes. I headed for the door, pulling at my own clothes as I went, trying to get them off and not end up falling in my rush. We both laughed like kids. He tried to dodge in front of me, his bare ass taunting my resolve not to grab him and run back to our bed. I gave him a playful push as he ran for the door. He caught me about the waist and spun me around, kissing me, distracting me as we turned, then dodged out the door ahead of me.

"Cheater!" I yelled as I sprinted out after him.

Andrew stood naked outside, the sun glinting off his golden, burnished skin in the afternoon light. The beauty of him standing there in all his glory, grinning at me, was enough to stop me in my tracks. Between that look and the warmth of love I could feel in his mind, I knew I was his world. The man was my god, and I'd joyfully worship him body and soul until the end of days. "Wow," I muttered.

He cocked his head to the side and wiggled his eyebrows impishly. A sudden wave of power washed over him. The change flowed like quicksilver, blurring the outline of his form and flowing smoothly as he shifted effortlessly from human to falcon. His body shimmered and shrunk in on itself, bronzed skin turning to glossy black feathers. Not wanting to be left behind, I let the change take me as well. I felt my body painlessly fold into itself and shrink to about a quarter of my size. My skin sprouted feathers, my arms transformed into wings, and my tail flowed out like an extension of my tailbone.

Catch me if you can! Andrew's laughter came out as a harsh *kak kak kak* as he launched himself into the sky. I took flight immediately after him. Soaring through the clouds, flying high, with the sun glinting off our shiny black feathers, we chased one another and danced in the air. We spun around each other, grasped talons, and whirled toward the ground with our wings folded against our backs, letting go at the last minute to spread our wings and glide over the grassy meadows mere inches above the ground. We reveled in exhilaration beyond words. Wings beating against the ether, soaring into the sky, whirling about, we were one with the wind and entirely fearless. No matter what anyone did, they wouldn't be able to take this away from us. Andrew might be tied to Stephon, but that damn vamp couldn't make him stay on the ground. Freedom abounded in the sky. Even if I could never release him from Stephon's control, he'd always be able to fly.

As we chased and played, mock hunting and sharpening our skills, the hours passed like water through a net. All too soon the sun began to sink toward the horizon, leaving the sky in twilight—an ever darkening indigo—and as the last of its warm rays glinted off our wings, we began a lazy, spiraling descent to earth. We floated almost directly above the cottage, where below us stood Max, my father-in-law, with two other people. One was a woman with dark hair and skin who wore a crinkled skirt and a white pullover blouse with drawstring ties at the neck; her wild hair, haphazardly frizzed about her head, was streaked with white. The other was a white-haired man with olive-toned skin and a hawkish nose framed by high cheekbones. Unlike Max and the woman, he hadn't aged gracefully; his skin was loose and bunched up on his neck, with wrinkles that sagged from the corners of unfriendly cold eyes. He dressed simply—in khakis and a dark-green T-shirt—yet carried himself with an air of self-importance.

I screeched a greeting to Max, who appeared nervous as he wiped an arm across his forehead. *Falcon eyes are great!* Andrew commented as we hovered among the thermals, slowly finding our way back to earth.

I chuckled, *Eyes that can see a mouse beneath meadow grass from a thousand feet in the air can easily see Max sweat under pressure. Time to help my father-in-law with his guests.*

The unknown man watched us carefully as we glided toward the ground. Andrew screamed in greeting to his father, who waved at us. With a sigh, I realized our time of peace had drawn to a close. I watched Andrew land gracefully at his father's feet, having sliced through the air as he quickly closed the distance. Not wanting to let go, I took a more reserved pace. I enjoyed the world consisting of only Andrew and myself, and I was reluctant to relinquish that freedom.

Come on. The sooner we land and see what they want, the quicker they'll leave and it will be just us again. Andrew understood, but what would be changed once they left?

I'm coming. I couldn't keep the grumble from my tone, even through our mental connection.

"Andrew." Max acknowledged the bird at his feet and then called to me. "Lance, come down, please. You have guests."

Chuuup. My contact call echoed across the meadow, answering Max's summons. I tucked my wings and dove to the ground before landing alongside Andrew. I clucked at Max and looked at the cottage door. Frowning slightly, Max opened the door, letting me hop into the cottage to shift and dress. Max, being born and raised a shifter, had little to no understanding of my awkward embarrassment with public nudity. I just couldn't bare it all in front of strangers, unlike most shape-shifters, who viewed nudity as a common state of life. Logically, I knew they were viewing my nude form when I was an animal, but then I was covered with fur or feathers. It was my human upbringing that made me different from the rest of my own kind. Max wasn't being difficult; he just didn't realize why I'd waited patiently for him to let me into the cottage.

Kak kak kak laughed Andrew's falcon at my discomfort as he followed me through the door. We transformed quickly. I gathered our clothes as I made my way to our bedroom and closed the door behind us. I tossed the clothes in the hamper in the corner and quickly grabbed a red sweater from the armoire, along with a pair of khakis and sneakers. Glancing in the mirror, I ran a comb through my wind tousled hair. Andrew had put on his usual jeans, black T-shirt, and sneakers. He took my hand and led me to the door so we could greet our guests.

"Please come in," Andrew said, smiling. Max clapped him warmly on the shoulder and then, as he passed, he placed a comforting hand on my shoulder as well. I shyly met the eyes of our guests as they shuffled in behind Max. They looked me over very carefully, sizing me up to see if they could spot any flaws. Andrew squeezed my hand in encouragement. I truly hated being looked at like a sideshow act. After meeting the vassals the other night and being totally ignored until they deigned to accept me as their "prince," and then having them size me up to see if I met their expectations, I really wasn't up for round two. I'd totally had it with feeling like a piece of choice prime rib on display at the meat market, surrounded by staring, starving people. I sighed softly and smiled up at Andrew, drawing strength from him, knowing it was unavoidable and would continue to be so for some time.

"Lance, this is Sandra Snow, the head of our family and clan." Andrew's voice was filled with respect. "She's the oldest in my family."

"Andrew, it's not nice to tell a lady's age," she scoffed at him, but she pulled him down so she could kiss him on the top of his head, like a wayward child. Then she turned a warm smile on me. "Welcome, Lance. Welcome to my family. And please, call me Sandy."

"Th-thank you," I stuttered, taken aback by her instant acceptance of me. I'd been prepared for disbelief and this kind woman offered approval. It took a minute to adjust.

"He's quite handsome, Andrew, but so shy. How will he ever handle your irrational outbursts? He'll need to be very strong to tame you," she teased me gently. My face grew hot as I blushed, but I met her gaze and let her see just a touch of the wolf inside. She blinked and laughed. "There's clearly more to him than appears at first glance."

Max then took over introductions as the tall elderly man entered the cottage. He looked around and then down his rather snooty nose on all of those before him. "This is Phillip Thomas Grey, a representative of the royal house. He's here to evaluate your claim to the royal bloodline. He is part of the royal family, albeit distantly. *Dr.* Carlson should be joining us shortly. He'll be bringing copies of the genetic tests results," Max announced just as the sound of tires on gravel signaled Tim's arrival.

"Won't you please have a seat?" Andrew motioned to the kitchen table, leading me around to one side. We sat close together, a united front.

Phillip Grey took a seat across from us. He looked at me skeptically, as if this was a grand waste of his time. I met his eyes unflinchingly, instinctively knowing that to show this man an iota of weakness would be a dire mistake. The wolf in me snarled at him, taking his stare as a direct challenge. Phillip's eyes grew wide and he immediately backed down, but was unable to look away. Sandy chuckled as she took a seat next to Andrew on the end, while Max sat directly opposite her.

"What is this?" Phillip demanded, still held captive by my wolf. "What do you have here, Max? What are you playing at?"

I smiled at his discomfort. My animal spirit snarled at the shadow of a creature hiding within the man's eyes. It told me the man before me was more human than shifter, despite the fact he claimed a royal heritage. This man was no threat to us, and we found him quite weak. Understanding filled me, and I realized Andrew had come to the same conclusion. I turned to smile up at him, releasing the man in the process. I leaned into Andrew; he wrapped an arm around my shoulders and I melted against his side.

The door opened and Tim entered, his shoes clicking on the hardwood, two file folders tucked beneath his arm. With a little kick, he closed the door behind him. Tim took the chair next to Phillip and placed the files on the table, then pushed one in front of Phillip and the other across the table to Sandy.

"I have confirmed Lance's test results. He *is* the son of Sasha Fenrir and Prince Henry Fitz. There is no doubt. The results are impeccable and can easily be duplicated, but I had them performed by three different, unrelated labs with the same exact result each time. He is a royal pureblood." Tim smiled and winked at me in encouragement.

"Impossible! They were killed in the first battle!" snarled Phillip Grey.

"No, Sasha and her protector, Prince Henry, fled the battle. My Lord Nathaniel sent her away, knowing he'd probably be killed, as our forces were outnumbered. We suspect he didn't want Sasha to see his death at her father's hands. She escaped with her protector, Prince Henry, who'd vowed to never leave her side," Tim said.

"What ridiculous lies!" Grey rolled his eyes.

"I was there. I'm a son of Lord Basil and a vassal to Lord Nathaniel. Through him, I'm vassal to Prince Lance." Tim's voice rose in volume as he continued over the sputtering Phillip

Grey. I did a double take when Tim referred to me as prince. We'd all kind of been avoiding the title, like it was the elephant in the room. When it came to Phillip Grey, though… there was an obvious need for it to be spoken aloud, no matter how uncomfortable it made me. I took a deep breath and tried to sit a bit straighter, hold my posture a bit more stiffly, as I imagined royals would, but really, how did I know? I'd never met any. Tim's voice, speaking with an authority I'd never thought to hear him use, brought me back to the conversation. "Regardless of whether you believe my story or not, the proof is in the test results. I made an extra copy for you to take to the royal family. I'm sure they'll want to see them and have them verified."

"This is outrageous. Who do you think you are?" he spat, snarling at me.

Andrew growled loudly and I placed a hand on his thigh. Pushing my chair back, I stood tall and proud, chin raised dominantly and without fear. I forced myself to accept who I was becoming, refusing to tremble. I let the wolf answer for me. He started as a low growl, ending in a roar that left Phillip Grey cowering in his chair.

"*I* am the son of Sasha and Prince Henry. *I* am myself, and no two-bit, self-proclaimed, snot-nosed little shadow of a beast like you will question me. If you have any doubts as to who I am, then I suggest you look within yourself and ask that little animal cowering in the shadows of your mind, because he has a much better understanding of who and what I am than you ever will. Have I made myself perfectly clear, Phillip Thomas Grey?" I never released him, staring into his eyes, my wolf demanding his submission. He shrank back as far from me as possible, twitching uncontrollably, exhibiting his fear. I'm sure he wished he could hide under the table. I could practically hear his beast whimpering. The skin seemed to move along his arms, the fur trying to break through as his beast fought for control—it wanted to crawl before me on its belly, beg for my forgiveness and acceptance, clearly recognizing me as dominant.

"Easy, boy," Sandy said, snickering. "He's liable to leave a puddle on the floor if you push him any further."

Andrew snaked his hand around my waist, totally relaxed despite my forceful handling of Phillip. Through our link, I could feel his enjoyment at my outburst. I took a deep breath before I sat back down. Andrew kept his arm around me, holding me close against his side. Without giving it a second thought, I dismissed Phillip outright as not even being worthy of my scorn.

"Andrew, I really like him." Sandy laughed, enjoying my bit of self-righteousness. "He bites."

Phillip Grey struggled to regain his composure. If he'd had any suspicions that my claims might've been falsified, he didn't seem to harbor them anymore. Andrew leaned in and nibbled on my ear to distract me. My beast still snarled, irritated at having this pathetic creature challenge us. Tim looked pleased. This bit of dominant behavior went against the grain for me. I didn't normally like confrontation, but my wolf would not abide being challenged in our own home.

"You said he has two shapes. I saw the falcon. What's the other?" Phillip seemed to have regained control of himself and dialed back his attitude to be much more subdued, if not entirely submissive. He'd chosen Max to speak to, as if he feared addressing me directly. The animal within me refused to let him get away with such evasiveness. If he wanted something from me, he needed to ask me.

"My other shape is a brown wolf," I answered him coolly. His gaze snapped to me and then away almost as quickly, but not before I saw his fear. My wolf liked the fear.

"I'll need to see it, if you don't mind. I need to make a complete report to the family." He stared at the edge of the table, refusing to meet my gaze.

"Fine, if you're sure you want to meet him." A warning growl vibrated through my chest. My frustration at being forced to put on a display for this bureaucrat, this man whose animal cowered in the dark, annoyed the animal spirit in me. I stood and walked into the bedroom, trying to put a lid on my emotions before I ripped the idiot's head off. Forcing myself to take care removing my clothes, I worked at retaining my fingers and not claws as the wolf tried to get free. Grey wanted a display and the wolf was going to give the man one he'd never forget. Once my clothes were folded and set aside, I allowed the wolf its freedom. I felt my form shimmer as the quicksilver took me, instantly melting and reshaping my body as a thick coat of dark-brown fur sprouted. The tail slid from my back as my spine elongated. With a vigorous shake, twisting from side to side, the last shiver of the transformation settled and I returned to the kitchen.

The fur along my back bristled indignantly and I jumped upon the tabletop, glaring at Phillip Grey. Waiting for any sign of a challenge, my wolf practically ached to put the aristocratic, self-righteous man in his place.

Andrew made no attempt to restrain me as I stood there, daring Phillip with my stare. I could show off with the best of them, first displaying one side, then turning around so Phillip could see the other. Sniffing as I leapt down from the table, I went straight to Andrew, put my front paws onto his lap, and pushed my head against his chest. Phillip rose, marched into the bedroom, and looked around, I guess to make sure I hadn't hidden in there or the bathroom.

"He didn't change in front of us," he hollered from the bedroom before rejoining us in the kitchen. "How do we know this isn't some ruse?" He glared at the wolf.

40

I found it totally incredulous that this little pipsqueak kept making challenges his beast didn't even have a snowball's chance in hell of answering. I growled at him, getting ready to attack. How dare he question me? The wolf jumped back on top of the table. He snarled at Grey, snapping his jaws as the man stumbled backward until he leaned against the wall. This time Andrew did have to grab hold of the wolf. How dare Grey question my integrity? Andrew had a tight grip on the scruff of my neck. I'd rip him apart, demand his submission in blood if he kept pushing me.

"Easy, Lance," Tim said, drawing my attention away from Phillip. "Can you show him, please? I know you aren't comfortable with public nudity. But he does seem insistent upon irrefutable proof."

I huffed at him and looked at Andrew. *Proof, huh? I'll give him his proof,* I told Andrew, who let go. I rubbed my head into his hands and he stood back, a knowing smile on his face. As the change began to take hold of me, I directed my change away from my human form. He wanted proof, and I refused to leave anything to chance. I felt my body fold in on itself, rising up from four legs to two, my snout forming into a beak, fur turning to black glossy feathers. I changed from wolf to falcon, leaving no doubt that I was both. Sandy clapped her hands and laughed uproariously at my choice of change.

"He's not giving you an inch, is he?" Sandy glared at Grey.

Max, who'd been silent, beamed with pride as my falcon flapped his wings, hopping awkwardly in the center of the table, wings outstretched. *Kak kak,* I screeched at Grey.

"There're those who've been able to shift into multiple animals for years who can't go from one beast to the next. They always have to be human in the middle." Max's voice was filled with awe.

Sandy got up and went into the bedroom. I folded my wings and stood proud but awkwardly on the slick tabletop. Talons were meant to wrap around branches, not stand on flat tables comfortably. I clacked my beak menacingly at Grey. Sandy emerged from the bedroom with a large towel, stopping to open it in his view. "Empty towel, Phillip, not big enough to hide in." Sandy snidely rolled her eyes as she handed it to Andrew. I fluttered onto Andrew's lap, taking a careful stand on his thigh, wary of my talons. I began to undo myself from the bird, returning to human. I changed slowly, controlling my shift so Andrew would be able to cover the essentials before my bits were flashed to the world. I let my legs slide to the floor as they lengthened, ending up sitting on Andrew's lap. I held onto my feathers as long as I could, trying to keep them for last. I'd returned almost completely to human before the feathers melted into my skin. Andrew draped the towel over my lap, protecting my modesty. I glared at Phillip Grey, contempt and anger flowing from me.

"Are you satisfied?" I asked him coldly.

He kept his eyes on the folder with the medical test results in front of him. "Yes. I am sorry, Your Highness. Please, forgive my insolence." He refused to look at me, every move he made perfectly submissive. It appeased the animal within me. He'd shamed himself and we both knew it. I carefully stood, wrapped the towel about my hips, and started toward the bedroom. Andrew stood to go with me, but Sandy shook her head and followed after me.

"Well, at least you know how to beg." Sandy's remark cut at Grey as she left the room, closing the door behind us. "Okay, you showed him. You were magnificent, by the way."

I warily watched her for a minute, then stepped into the bathroom and closed the door between us while she began searching through the armoire for fresh clothes. I stared at my reflection in the mirror, trying to regain control of my scattered emotions.

"Thank you, I guess," I mumbled loud enough to be heard through the door.

She softly knocked and I opened the door a crack. "Here, I've found you some clothes." She handed me a pair of tailored blue slacks and a white flowing poet shirt with a deep V-neckline and white laces. I eyed the shirt skeptically. It was still semicasual, but much more ostentatious than anything I'd ever worn. My wardrobe before Andrew consisted of Goodwill and thrift store finds.

"You want me to wear this?" I eyed the clothes warily, rather surprised by Sandy's selection. With a sigh, I closed the door again, placed the clothes on the counter, and began dressing.

Sandy pointedly ignored my comment. "I know he's a little kiss-ass, but you need him—even if he is a complete waste of space and can barely hold an animal form for more than ten minutes. You need to charm him so he'll agree to present you to the court. If he drags his feet, or if he decides he doesn't like you and refuses to put your name before the family, then we lose before we even get started. He can't keep you from the court permanently—not with skills like yours—but he *can* delay things. It would be better to have his support."

Once dressed, I opened the bathroom door. "Charm him? I don't know how to be charming." I looked at Sandy, trying not to panic. "I know how to be shy and silent. The wolf handles aggression and dominance. Nobody said anything about being charming." Somehow, I had to smooth that jackass's ruffled feathers.

"Sweethcart, everyone born in this world has charm."

"Not me. I have anger and dysfunction issues."

Sandy gave a put-upon sigh. "Okay, here's what you do. He acknowledges you as a prince. So pretend to be a confused airhead." I groaned as she continued. "It's pretty well known that his taste runs to men and he thinks rather highly of himself. Flatter him and make him feel good about himself. He's a puffed up know-it-all, so let him think you admire him for something—anything at all. Whatever subject he brings up and talks about like he's an authority, let him have his moment. If he thinks a real royal pureblood prince regards him as important, then it'd be to his benefit to get you acknowledged by the royal family. He'd come away with more status—or so he'd like to think. The family knows exactly what he is, which is why they sent him on this errand in the first place."

"I don't know about this. After pushing him around out there, don't you think he'll be suspicious if I start playing stupid now?" I frowned and headed back into the bathroom. Sandy followed and handed me a comb. I began to work it through the length of my hair, trying to get it into some semblance of normalcy instead of bushing out all over the place.

"You really are quite striking," she said as she looked me over from head to toe before nodding to herself over some decision she'd made. "The man isn't bright enough to be suspicious of anything that isn't spelled out for him."

I looked into the mirror critically, trying to see myself as she did and found myself rather surprised by my reflection. My curly brown hair hung in loose locks, framing my face, and the time spent outdoors had bronzed my complexion. Between the open laces of the shirt, my rather well-muscled pecs showed through. I'd tucked the shirttails into the waistband of the blue slacks. It wasn't a look I'd have chosen for myself, but I couldn't say I hated it.

"It's not the perfect seduction outfit, but you do look very handsome. Now go bat your eyelashes, flirt like hell, and blush a lot when he talks," Sandy said, fluttering her eyelashes at me.

I sighed and walked out into the bedroom and grabbed my black boots from beside the armoire.

"I'd also recommend you sit on Andrew's lap, because he's liable to get a bit irritated with this performance," she added.

I'm not sure I can do this, I sent to Andrew, anxiety building up as I prepared to go back out into the kitchen.

Take Sandy's counsel seriously. If she's recommending something, I'm sure she has her reasons. Tim's going over the medical tests with Grey now… not that he's understanding any of it. Andrew's mental chuckle calmed my frayed nerves.

She wants me to flirt with him. I couldn't prevent the disgust from coloring my tone. *I'm supposed to make him feel… I don't know… better about me, I guess. She says to "charm him,"* I grumbled.

I don't like it, but…. I could feel Andrew's hesitation. *Do it.*

I looked at Sandy and strengthened my resolve, then took hold of the bedroom door handle. "I can do this," I assured myself. I took a deep breath, opened the door, and returned to the kitchen, where the others were waiting.

Andrew had turned halfway around in his chair, to see me when I walked back into the room. His jaw dropped partway open with surprise when he saw me. A certain hunger I'd come to recognize flashed through his eyes, so clearly he approved of the outfit. I'd never worn anything other than jeans and T-shirts around him, so I guess it *was* a bit of a shock. Good thing Phillip Grey had reclaimed his seat across the table from him, so Andrew's back was to him. He missed Andrew picking his jaw up off the floor.

"Now, behave like gentlemen." Sandy nudged me forward toward Andrew, then reclaimed her seat. I put a gentle hand on Andrew's chest, and he pulled me down onto his lap. His arms were like steel bands wrapped around my waist. I liked the possessive feelings coming from Andrew; it gave me strength to know I belonged to him.

You look absolutely stunning, he whispered into my mind, licking the outer edge of my ear gently. I shivered a bit and leaned back against him appreciatively.

When Phillip finally grasped the concept and nodded after extensive explanation, I spoke up. Cringing internally at the mental picture of a bubbleheaded valley girl, I was unable to prevent myself from feeling incredibly stupid.

"Wow, Phillip, I'm glad you understand the test results. They're way beyond me." Three men looked at me with varying degrees of stunned disbelief in their expressions. But Phillip preened under my praise.

"Th-thank you, Your Highness," he stammered.

Max looked confused, but Tim caught on immediately. When he met my eyes, he winked slightly. He asked about the news at the royal court, and Phillip prattled on about various cousins who—in his eyes—were making fools of themselves with some contrivance or another. Clearly in his element, he expounded court gossip at great length, and I pretended to pay rapt attention. I asked questions about this cousin or that and agreed with every word he said. The whole affair left me feeling disgusted and in need of a shower. It was hard to believe how shallow and ignorant the man was.

Andrew's body temperature had begun to rise, and I could fccl the heat emanating from him in waves and hear his heartbeat accelerating. *What are you doing?* Andrew's growling voice sounded in my mind. He'd tried to draw away from me, but I discreetly held onto his arms beneath the table, needing his support to continue this charade.

It's an act, remember? I'm supposed to charm him. The frustration and humiliation of having to act even more ignorant than Phillip, and how dirty it made me feel to have to hide who I really was yet again, flowed from me to Andrew. I began rubbing soft circles on the back of his hand with my thumb, trying inconspicuously to console my possessive mate, while still flattering Grey the idiot. I leaned forward with an elbow on the table, resting my head on my hand. I batted my eyelashes at Phillip and acted as though his words were the most important thing I'd ever heard. I wanted to vomit.

Phillip went on, gushing at my attention, telling me every secret he'd ever learned. All the while, I smiled wider than any bimbo schoolgirl I'd ever seen. In a dark corner in my mind, the wolf in me gagged. Time seemed to drag on mercilessly, and I feared I wouldn't be able to keep this up for much longer without having to excuse myself.

Finally, Tim rescued me. "Well, lady and gentlemen, I think it's getting late. I need to be getting back to my office."

"Yes, Laura will have dinner on the table by now and will be concerned that I haven't returned. Can I interest you in staying for dinner?" Max looked first to Sandy, then included Grey in his invitation.

"That sounds wonderful, but I really must be getting back." Sandy smiled at Max.

"Ah yes, I do suppose I must be leaving as well." Phillip seemed to stumble a bit, unsure what he should be doing.

The relief I felt was short-lived, because when I sat back against Andrew's chest, I could feel his anger; his skin was hot to the touch, feverish with the control he was exerting to prevent himself from disemboweling Grey. His hands trembled beneath mine on my lap, his nails having shifted to claws. The rage and desire to rip Phillip apart seeped through our link. Trying to pacify him, I began to pet Andrew's arm. He'd been keeping his feelings from me, shielding me from how tortured my flirting with another man in front of him made him feel. Even though he knew Grey disgusted me, it clearly infuriated him.

Sandy winked at me, nodding. At least someone was pleased with my performance. Phillip lived in a world of his own importance and had believed every fake compliment and smile. Our guests got to their feet and began moving toward the door.

I climbed to my feet and drew Andrew up with me. I could feel his wolf snarling as he grabbed me, leaving not an inch between us, his erection pressed hard against my ass. His beast was laying claim and wouldn't allow me to get away. With his arms wrapped tightly around my waist, I held his hands securely in my own as I leaned back against his chest. The contact soothed us both. His rapid breathing began to slow to a pace that matched my own. *Easy, love, I belong only to you,* I sent back with every iota of love and devotion in my heart.

Mine! That was the only sentiment I received in return, which was fine. In an odd way, just that one word meant the world to me. He wouldn't let anyone take me from him, especially not some pompous fool like Phillip.

We followed our guests to the door. "It was nice to meet you, Phillip. I enjoyed talking with you and hearing about all our cousins. You'll have to come and visit us again." I treated him as an equal, even though he could never be my equal when it came to the beast inside.

He preened and bowed smartly. "Prince Lance, you honor me. I'll present the good news to the family. I'm sure they'll send for you soon. Maybe I'll be able to escort you myself."

"That'd be very pleasant." I smiled at him, leaning farther into Andrew's embrace, against his chest. Andrew stood haughtily stiff behind me. I could feel the vibration of the silent growl deep in the pit of his stomach as he pressed against my back. Max and Tim escorted Phillip out between them, leaving me alone with Andrew and Sandy.

"Beautiful performance, child. That peacock will be gushing praise for you all over the royal family. I told you we all have charm, and you're no different. You've got a real prize here, Andrew. You chose better for this family than any match I could've ever found for you. You have my blessings and then some." Sandy kissed me on the cheek and patted a startled Andrew on the shoulder. "He'll be okay, child," she whispered to me. "Just reassure him you only belong to him. Love each other." Sandy snickered, then kissed a stunned Andrew upon the cheek before ducking out the door.

"Thank you," I called after her. "Good night."

"That was quite the performance," Andrew grumbled as we went back into our little cottage and closed the door on the night. I led him over to our favorite armchair, and Andrew pulled me down onto his lap.

"You know I just tried to do what Sandy asked me to." I just wanted to curl up with my mate and forget the whole distasteful thing.

"To be honest, love, it doesn't matter why you were doing it or that I understood the logic behind it. I just wanted to rip him apart. The more you flattered him, the bloodier I imagined his corpse to be." I felt Andrew's lips on my neck, then his teeth biting at the skin behind my ear. "You belong to me."

"You're right. I belong to only you."

"I couldn't believe you were paying so much attention to his nonsense. Claiming you didn't understand the test results, especially after listening to Tim go through them in painstaking detail over and over." Andrew twitched slightly, but his temperature had returned to normal and his heartbeat had slowed as he comforted himself by brushing his hands along my arms. The touch of my skin pacified his beast more than anything else.

"You're my mate. The only person I'm interested in is you. I'll do anything to free you, including fake interest in some pompous blue blood. Believe me, the whole time my wolf sat in the back of my mind, throwing up." I chuckled softly. Andrew growled his approval, nipping at my collarbone. I hummed in pleasure, tipping my head in submission to my mate, offering him more of my neck. "I love only you."

"You look so beautiful tonight." He buried a hand in my hair, letting the curls slide through his fingers.

"Sandy chose the outfit," I told him, having some trouble putting words together. His attentions were igniting the lust that always simmered in my veins for him. Andrew thought I looked beautiful—sexy or handsome would have been preferred, but coming from Andrew I didn't mind.

He ran a finger down from my neck to my shoulder, tracing a line down my arm to my waist. His light touch set my skin on fire. My breathing became ragged, and I reached for him. He caught my hands in his, lifted them over my head, and held them at the wrist. I offered no resistance.

He smiled, leaving whisper-soft kisses against my neck. His hot breath raised goose bumps along my skin. "You tortured me all afternoon. Now you're mine alone, and I want to make sure you never forget how well I can hold your attention." As he gently laughed, the vibration sent shivers of anticipation dancing through my body, drawing a wanton moan from my lips. Andrew eased out from under me and pressed me back into the chair while he hovered over me. He lazily left a line of hot, wet kisses following the neckline of the shirt, then raked his teeth against my collarbone and nibbled at my skin as he followed it down to meet the other side. Rolling my head to the side, I panted softly as his kisses dipped along my sternum before rising again with the flow of the material up across my other collarbone, up my neck to nibble on my other ear.

His kisses flowed along my jaw until his lips captured mine with a growl. I opened my mouth to his demands, darting my tongue out to taste his lower lip and trace the outline. When he released my hands, I dug them into his hair, clinging to him. I desperately needed him, and he needed to reclaim me as his own. He slipped one of his hands inside my slacks to stroke my hardening cock.

"Andrew," I gasped as he closed his fist around the head of my erection.

Andrew stood, pulling me to my feet. "It's time to take this to the bedroom, my love." I swayed slightly, as if my legs had the consistency of melted rubber, but Andrew was there to steady me. I leaned on him, my rock… the one sure thing in my life. Together we moved into the bedroom amid soft gentle kisses as we reestablished our claims on each other. Our souls were one. Nothing could stand between us.

CHAPTER 4

IT WAS late… or early, depending on how you looked at it. Dawn was on the verge of making itself known, but had yet to penetrate the darkness. There was a bit of a chill in the air as I rolled over in bed to discover myself alone. Embers glowed in the fireplace, casting a bit of light and warmth about the room. Andrew had obviously gotten up. I listened carefully, but could not hear him. He wasn't in the bathroom or out in the kitchen—I couldn't imagine where he'd gotten to.

Andrew? I sent through our mental link. I could feel he was close by.

I'll be back in a minute. Stephon is on the phone. Andrew's frustration could be felt through our link.

What did that damn vamp want now? I tried to calm down. Getting pissed off would only bother Andrew more. I climbed from the bed and walked through to the kitchen, then out the door. Once outside, I found Andrew seated at our old table, now our picnic table, cell phone in hand.

"Really…. Come on, Stephon. There's no chance…. No. I said *no*." Andrew practically snarled at the vamp. "Listen to me.

I'm not bringing him to you so you can make him one of your beneficiaries. He's free and he's staying that way."

I closed my eyes and took a deep calming breath. It had always been a possibility that one of the vamps would expect me to become property. Ultimately, if that was what it took to keep Andrew, I'd do it in a heartbeat. Granted, my vamp owner would never know what hit him because I'd be less than a model slave. But if it meant being tied to this place and I got to keep Andrew… yeah, it wouldn't be all that bad.

"Stephon, he is so. You've got Tim's findings sitting in front of you," Andrew continued to argue. "Really… Tim? You think he's an instigator to free shape-shifters and start a war? Man, you need to get down off that mountain; your brains have leaked out your ears. Tim's the biggest pacifist I know." A pause…. The stupid vamp must have been arguing.

"I know you've known him longer than I have. But that doesn't mean…."

I could hardly believe what I was hearing. Stephon actually believed that Tim—sweet Dr. Tim—would want to instigate a shifter rebellion? The vamp obviously didn't know Tim at all.

"Stephon, you've lost your mind. Maybe you need to hibernate for a while until your sanity returns. It's late. I'm going back to bed with my mate. When you recover your mind, I'll call you and we can talk again. Until then, leave me and my family alone. We haven't done anything to get your tail in a twist, and our family elder has approved my mating, so move on." Andrew shook his head as he hung up the phone. I could feel the splitting jab of pain Stephon pounded into Andrew's mind.

"Ahh!" Andrew cried out, putting his hands to his temples. I ran to him and placed my hands over his. He stared into my eyes, pain tearing through both our minds.

"This ends. *Now*." I nodded as I sought out the connection between my mate and the vampire torturing him. I had no idea how to free him, but my wolf seemed to know instinctively. I let the wolf hunt down the connection, saw him following the pain back into the depths of Andrew's mind. It followed the pain and the memories, starting with the most recent, then back from there until I could see scenes of Andrew's childhood flashing before our eyes.

The pain increased in both our minds, as if Stephon knew what we were doing, knew I was hunting him. It only made the wolf angrier.

"I c-can't take much more…," Andrew panted. His skin had gone clammy in my hands, and his heartbeat was becoming erratic.

"Just hold on a bit longer. I can see it now." I reached for what appeared to be threads of light. They were stretched tautly between the vamp and Andrew, a spiderweb weaving and flowing through Andrew's mind, attached to a multitude of his past memories. Each connection was alive with energy, straining and ripping at my mate's mind.

My wolf grabbed hold of the connection flowing into Andrew's mind before it could spread further through his memories. With a mental yank, I pulled back on the threads, and although it relieved some of the pressure, it still didn't break. *MINE!* The wolf screamed along the connection, sending waves of pain like rending teeth and ripping talons back at Stephon. Then the wolf set his teeth to the strands, severing the connection with one swift bite.

Andrew slumped forward into my arms, resting his forehead on my shoulder. *Mine,* my wolf crooned. I could feel him nuzzling Andrew, relaxing away the last remnants of pain.

Yours. Andrew's mental reply was a bit weak, but there nonetheless. Never again would I allow someone to hold his mind hostage. I'd only tolerate him possessing a link as mentally intimate as this with me. I wasn't into sharing.

As I slid my fingers through Andrew's hair, massaging his scalp, trying to ease the last of the stress from my mate, I could feel his shock and surprise as the tie to his master didn't reappear—and his relief. Never again would Stephon be able to send him pain. Granted, this in no way freed him of his bondage with Stephon, but with the mental hold cut, the first of many ties had been severed. My wolf howled with joy.

"He's gone." Andrew's voice trembled with a mixture of anxiety and relief.

"Yes, and he'll never have that kind of hold on you ever again."

"I… I don't know what to do. Stephon's always been with me."

"It's okay. I'm with you now." Andrew rested his hands on my hips, tightening his grip. The phone, which Andrew had dropped when Stephon's assault had begun, started ringing from its spot in the grass beside the table. I picked it up and turned it off.

"You shouldn't turn it off. What if Dad needs us at the ranch?" Andrew clung to me, rubbing his face into my shoulder.

"They'll be fine for a while. The sun will be up soon. Let's head back to bed. We can go hunting and visit your family in the morning. We'll deal with it all later."

"Yeah, sounds good." Andrew sighed. He radiated physical exhaustion as he placed an arm over my shoulders and we went back into the cottage, to rest in our bedroom.

CHAPTER 5

WE SLEPT in. The day dawned through our curtainless windows and we'd rolled over and kept right on sleeping, sunlight be damned. Andrew looked like he was getting the first good night's sleep he'd had in years. I'd never realized how stressful being connected to a vampire had been for him. During the day, he stayed up with me, while his nights were shared with Stephon. His sleep must have been fitful, at best.

When I awoke, I was tempted… oh, how I was tempted… to crawl between the sheets and give Andrew a blowjob he wouldn't forget, but I decided to let him sleep. There'd be plenty of time for that later. Right now, my man needed his rest.

I planted a featherlight kiss on his forehead and crept from our bed, made a pit stop in the bathroom, and then sought out the kitchen. I had just put the kettle on the stove to make tea when I went to turn around, only to realize Andrew stood directly behind me. He kissed me, sucking on the pulse point behind my ear. *So much for letting my man sleep.*

"Don't need more sleep. Just you in my arms," Andrew mumbled, nipping at my earlobe. He spun me around and locked his lips on mine; my toes curled and I dug my fingers into his bare shoulders.

"I want to go hunting." Andrew's sleep-softened voice tickled against my kiss-swollen lips.

"As if I could deny you anything after a kiss like that." I panted, trying to catch my breath. If there was one skill my man had mastered, it was kissing. Andrew was a kissing icon. He should have a bronze statue erected, something proclaiming his prodigious skill.

"I'll build the fires in the fireplaces so the house will stay warm. The days have been remaining cool lately." With that, he let go of me and made his way over to the fireplace. I turned on the stereo and searched out some fun music: "Werewolves of London." I couldn't help but dance to the song. Andrew laughed at my antics and happiness as I sang along with the music. After adding fresh wood to the remaining embers and putting the grates back in place, he joined me. He swayed his hips from side to side, bumping against me as we sang along with the music. When the song ended, we went out to the front yard, still laughing as we transformed into our wolves.

It'd been a gradual thing, something I'd been noticing about his beasts ever since our mating. I thought they'd grown larger, but in the morning sun there was no longer any doubt in my mind of our shared power. His wolf had definitely increased in size, appearing a good couple inches taller as well as heavier, more muscular. Andrew's wolf had always been impressive, but his beast had become massive and had even changed color. He'd lost the gray that once mottled his coat and now displayed a pure snow-white pelt—he was simply magnificent. His transitions had become effortless, instantaneous, and pain-free. Our bonding had done wonders for both of us. I no longer questioned or doubted his love, and he'd truly become my alpha. We both took off at a run, playing as wolves. We hunted and brought down a large elk.

We howled at the top of our lungs, our joy filling the morning air. In the distance, we heard the twins bay in answer to our call. As one we yipped and sang back. We tucked into the elk and ate our fill, devouring most of the large animal. Then we took off full tilt, racing around our meadow, simply reveling in being together.

We were almost back to the cottage when I caught the whiff of another large predator. The heavy, oily, musky scent of bear clung to the wind. I didn't recognize the scent, but Andrew did. Uncle David had come to call and he wasn't in human form, but stood in our meadow as a large black bear. My wolf snarled at his intrusion. This predator had no right to be in *my* territory without *my* permission. Andrew telepathically reasoned he was probably here to check on him because I'd cut Andrew's mental link with Stephon. Honestly, I didn't care whether Stephon had sent David or not—I didn't like the man and I wanted him out of my territory. He was ruining a perfectly good morning with his trespassing, regardless of whether our private time was fleeting or not. I knew David from Andrew's memories as a bully, one who'd hurt my man repeatedly. I also knew he had a lot of nerve showing himself here without calling first. It was the height of rudeness to enter territory not your own without an invitation.

We took up a position between the bear and the door to our cottage. He stood on his hind legs, roaring and pawing at the air, putting on a display of dominance. I could tell David enjoyed throwing his weight around, but Andrew's larger wolf was nearly the same size. David might be a bear, but he was far from the largest black bear I'd ever seen. It was time for David to learn some manners. I could feel myself shifting ever so slightly, just as I had done with the assassin drones—Fangs elongated and claws thickened, both becoming longer, sharper, and deadlier. I snarled back at the bear, accepting his challenge. I inserted myself between Andrew and the bear. I could feel myself bristling for the attack, gnashing my teeth, preparing to give the bear a beating he'd never forget. Memories of what Andrew had endured at this man's hand filled my mind. The mental image of his laughing face as he punished Andrew enraged me further. Andrew's fear spilled through our mental link as the bear took a clumsy swipe at me.

Before I could retaliate, Andrew began to change—and he sure wasn't getting any smaller. It took a moment for the shock to pass through me as his form solidified into an enormous polar bear, towering over me as it roared at the black bear. Andrew stood almost twice the size of his uncle's bear, with paws the size of my head and claws that looked like daggers. To say I quickly got out of his way would be putting it mildly. A sound like a thunderclap echoed through the meadow as the polar bear clubbed the black bear, which sent David tumbling down the drive. Seeing the bear rolling might've been amusing if I couldn't feel how totally terrified Andrew was of the man.

The black bear practically leapt to its feet as it tried to get away from Andrew, lumbering down the drive with a significant limp, bleeding from the gashes running down its shoulder. Andrew gave chase as far as the tree line, with me right behind him. As David hustled down the drive heading for the ranch, I turned my attention to Andrew, hoping my mate was still inside the giant bear. He stood at the tree line, growling and huffing, pounding the ground with his front paws. He tossed his head violently left and right as he roared his triumph and dared David to cross him again. It was a glorious spectacle of primal strength and power, and I was both in awe of and terrified for my mate at the same time.

Andrew? I felt a stream of emotions washing from him, ranging from rage to pride. My wolf whined in concern, but the transformation had been as smooth from wolf to bear, as effortless, as his first shift to wolf had been. He was practically giddy, like a schoolkid getting back some of his own from the bully. He'd finally gotten to take a swipe at David, and he'd defended me in the process.

He lumbered around the field, grunting with ursine laughter as he displayed his strength by breaking off branches from the trees, surprised as all get-out at his own strength. I watched him at play and wanted to join in. Next thing I knew, the quicksilver of a shift had begun and I'd become a polar bear as well. The ease of the shift startled me—all it took was a simple thought. There was no need for deep concentration or any extra effort, and it came without pain. This was what our joined power had ultimately given us both. We nosed and hugged each other, though our large clawed paws made them more like pats on the back than real hugs. We ran around the clearing, chasing after each other, playing like cubs.

It didn't take but half an hour before two sandy wolves came running up the path toward the cottage. The twins, either under orders from Max or having snuck out, had arrived. Knowing Andrew's brothers, they'd found out about Uncle David facing off against a polar bear and had come to see it for themselves. What they found was not one, but two polar bears romping around our little meadow. We let them join our play, careful not to hurt the young wolves, as we were nearly three times their size. They happily joined us, nipping at our heels and running circles around us, obviously feeling no pity for Uncle David's pain.

It was long past noon when first Andrew, then I, felt comfortable enough to transform back to human. We lumbered toward the cottage, shifted, and went inside. I emerged after having donned a pair of sweatpants and waved to the boys to join us. They looked at each other, then barked in unison as they came running. Andrew met them at the door, holding extra sweats.

Our joining had definitely done something for our ability to transform. I knew I wouldn't need to practice my tiger for him to be magnificent. Plus, the amount of time in which I needed to remain the beast in order to be comfortable with the new form was much less than it had been before.

"That was totally awesome!" Joe expounded once he'd transformed, waving his hands excitedly. "Nobody's been able to give Uncle David a beating in ages! He came back whimpering like a pup. I wonder what he's going to tell Stephon? You gotta tell us, who clobbered him?"

I laughed. "Andrew did. He transformed into a polar bear to protect me because I wanted to attack him as a wolf. I still think I could've taken him."

"Sure, love, and given me heart failure in the process. Besides, I kind of like that bear… the polar bear, I mean. He's strong and totally fearless." Andrew grinned from ear to ear. "I think when it comes to brute force, that bear is pretty unstoppable."

"Yeah, and don't forget enormous." Grinning like a fool, I took the kettle from the stove and filled it with water for tea.

"Well, you two have been incommunicado for so long, and then Stephon started yelling about something being wrong and not being able to reach you. Dad figured, after David came back limping, he'd best send us up to check things out and make sure you didn't need us to contact Tim," Jack gushed. "We never guessed you'd be able to cut Stephon out of the loop. He insisted you must be hurt or dying because you couldn't possibly have cut him off yourself." He roared with laughter as he filled us in on everything we'd missed.

"Oh yes, I could and *did*." I rolled my eyes and grabbed a mug from the cabinet. "Anyone else want tea?" A chorus of no came from the rest of the guys.

"You cut him out?" Joe asked incredulously. "Good for you. Crappy, eavesdropping, Peeping-Tom vampire got what's good for him, sticking his nose where it doesn't belong."

I chuckled, because that was exactly how I felt about him, more than a little indignant that he'd dare to hurt Andrew in an attempt to force his will on him because he didn't like me.

"Well, I guess this means the honeymoon's over," I sighed, casting a loving look at Andrew.

"Okay, if you two are gonna get mushy, we're out of here," Jack protested, but he made no move to get up from the table. I laughed and cuffed him upside the back of his head. Affection for Jack and Joe filled my heart, and I shared the feeling with Andrew. The two juveniles soothed an ache in me for all the failed sibling relationships I'd tried to create over the years with other foster kids. Peace, happiness, and just a bit of pride for his little brothers resonated from him at my acceptance of them. I knew I'd never be whole without him.

"We really had better get back to the farm before Dad comes looking for us." Joe stood up, nudging Jack to his feet.

"We'll call Tim and then come down to the house," Andrew told the twins as he escorted them out the door. After a quick shift, the twins took off in the direction of the farm. The sound of barking faded as they disappeared down the road. Andrew came back in carrying the extra pairs of sweat pants and sighed.

"Time's up, love." After grabbing his cell phone from the counter beside the door, he turned it on and called Tim.

"Hey, Tim, it's Andrew."

Andrew, how are things? Is everything all right? Andrew shared Tim's part of the conversation through our link. There were times the mental connection seemed very strange, such as hearing a phone conversation—but not really *hearing* the other party—yeah, odd. Not every single thought or heard word my mate experienced was shared. We both had some semblance of privacy and control over what we sent to the other, but when we made love and our souls united, all our experiences were shared in that moment. So even if something was held back, it would eventually be shared. Then there were moments like this, when the echo of the conversation rang through my mind and it just felt strange.

"Fine, everything is fine. We are fabulous," Andrew reassured our concerned doctor.

So what can I help you with?

"We've had a couple of interesting developments and will be heading down to the farm. Want to meet us there? Then we can fill everyone in at once."

When do you want to meet?

"We should be there in about half an hour. That work for you?" Andrew suggested.

Half an hour… yes that should be fine. Let me give Charlie a call and see if she can join us as well.

"Okay, sounds great, Tim. See you in a few."

While Andrew talked with Tim, I caught a whiff of myself and decided I needed a shower and fresh clothes. No sense in looking or smelling like we'd just been rolling around in the dirt, even though we pretty much had been. If we hurried, there'd be just enough time for a quick shower. I left the kitchen, stripped off my sweatpants, and tossed them in the hamper along the way.

I started the water running and had just stepped in when Andrew joined me. The large multihead shower was a luxury, and money well spent in my book. Though a slick wet Andrew was a huge distraction, we were able to scrub each other down and wash our hair in no time. I itched to take hold of him and find our blissful release.

I want you too, but we have guests coming to the ranch, Andrew whispered through our link. At his rebuff, I leaned back against him provocatively, feeling Andrew's hard cock as it rubbed between the cheeks of my ass. I could feel the lust and want pouring from him.

Maybe just a quickie? I suggested, grinding and wiggling my hips from side to side, which elicited a moan of desire. Andrew settled his hands on my hips, stilling my efforts; he set his teeth against my throat.

"No such thing as a quickie with you. You are *so* bad." His tone belied the chastisement in his words as he pushed me up against the shower tiles. "Teasing me like this really isn't fair," he growled, sliding his erection between my asscheeks. "You feel so good, I want to take you up on your invitation… but we can't very well leave my parents to entertain our vampire guests. I promise you, leannan, I'll make sure you come on my cock… very soon." A gentle kiss on my shoulder ended with the sharp pinch of teasing teeth and a snicker, before he turned off the water, abandoning me in the shower. He threw a towel at me before hastening his exit from the room.

"Aw, now that's not fair," I grumbled, catching the towel before it hit the wet floor. I dried off, my cock achingly hard.

"Tim will be arriving at the ranch before us if you don't get a move on. It'd be nice to let them know he's coming before he shows up on their doorstep, especially since he's bringing that warrior woman with him," Andrew called from the bedroom.

I chuckled as I quickly ran a comb through my hair. "Yeah, your mother might not appreciate Charlie without an introduction."

Andrew stepped up behind me, took the comb, and began running it through my hair. "I love the feeling of your hair between my fingers."

Reaching back, I took hold of him by his waist and pushed my rear into his hips, swaying. "I love the feel of you pressed against me," I practically purred.

"Just a little payback, love. I'm already regretting leaving the cottage and we haven't even left yet." His eyes rolled and he moaned softly. With a laugh, I took the comb away from him. I felt his half-hard cock stiffen behind me, and I loved knowing I had that effect on him.

"Dangerous. I always knew you were dangerous," he said as I sprinted from the bathroom, with him following, to stand in front of the armoire so I could dig out some clothes. I ended up in jeans and a blue sweater. Andrew also wore jeans, but he'd chosen a button-down gray shirt.

You look hot. My heart practically skipped a beat, my libido reminding me of my still throbbing need.

"Thank you, my love. I think you look pretty gorgeous yourself." He took me in his arms and nibbled at my ear. Now it was my turn to sigh and melt into him, my own arousal just as evident as his.

"Obviously I'm not the only dangerous one in this cottage," I whispered.

He chuckled as he grabbed my hand and we rushed out the door. We'd just make it to the farm in time—if we hurried. We took off running for the tree line.

I think I'm going to want a garage so we can keep a vehicle here. We should probably think about some type of central heating as well. The fireplaces are nice for now, but when the temps plunge in winter, we'll have the plumbing to consider. We don't want to deal with frozen pipes. Andrew's thoughts rambled on as he planned for our future at the cottage, and it relaxed me. It pulled me away from the increasing nervousness I was beginning to feel as we neared the ranch.

I enjoyed being able to have a silent conversation with Andrew. It allowed me to listen to the animals in the woods without disturbing them and still have a dialogue. It was the best of both, nature and talking with my love. I could share my convictions and thoughts about the vampires' manipulation and control of the shape-shifters—it truly bordered on slavery, and it set my very teeth on edge.

I just don't understand it. How can a race as strong as ours give up everything it means to be part of the wild? I grumbled.

It was a war. In the end, it isn't the loser who sets terms. Andrew's reply made sense, but at the same time it went against everything I'd been told about his "good" vampire master.

If vamps care so much about us, then why hurt us? Why rip apart mated pairs and families? If we lived independently as allies for so long, why cripple us and claim we are incapable of caring for ourselves?

You have to understand. After the war, there were so few left....

I know the rhetoric you grew up with, but there's no way you can tell me that Sandy, Max, and your mom aren't capable of taking care of themselves. Maybe at one time it might have been necessary, maybe keeping records so families wouldn't accidentally cross bloodlines or something. But the way the vampires mentally tie you to them and can force their will under duress and threat of pain—it's slavery.

It was so wrong. If our people became extinct because we couldn't take care of ourselves, then we deserved to go extinct. The very idea that a people so strong and vibrant couldn't take care of themselves bordered on the ridiculous, and I believed it to be a load of crap.

I know you don't understand. I'm probably not explaining it very well. I could feel Andrew's frustration at my lack of understanding. But from an outside perspective, it was overt control, plain and simple. Still, society be damned—my main concern was Andrew and his family. I wanted them to be safe and free to make their own choices. I didn't want Stephon deciding who little Angela was going to mate with just to make stronger shifters. I wanted her to have the right to fall in love, just like any other person. If I had to become some sort of royalty in order to ensure she got to choose, then I'd do it for Andrew.

Too soon, we arrived at the farm, holding hands. Together we ran up the porch steps and through the front door. It seemed we were in luck, as Tim hadn't arrived. Unfortunately, Uncle David hadn't left yet. From outside we could hear raised voices coming from the house. When we entered the kitchen, Max stood toe to toe with David, both of them yelling at the top of their lungs. Laura sat at the table, in tears. I went instantly to her side and wrapped an arm around her shoulders as she turned to hide her face. I snarled a warning at David. His eyes grew wide as he noticed Andrew and I had walked in the door.

"What are you still doing here?" Andrew spoke, his voice deadly, soft, and even. "I thought I had made myself pretty clear. Get the hell out of my territory, David."

"You're gonna feel my lash again, you brat!" hissed David.

"Try it and you'll be dead before you can raise the leather." I looked him in the eyes, enforcing the challenge in my threat, as the wolf came out in full force. Nobody pushed my family around, and I'd had enough of this guy. "Keep it up, David, and I'll have your bear for lunch." I snapped my teeth menacingly at him.

"Who the hell are you anyway?" David backed away from me as far as he could get, the stove putting an end to his flight.

I felt a hand on my shoulder. It was Tim; they must have arrived right behind us. Charlie took up a position between David and everyone else. Whip in hand, she glared at David, daring him to transform just so she'd have an excuse to let the lash ring out.

"He's Prince Marcus Lance Fenrir Fitz," stated Tim. "If you proceed to accost him, his mate, or their family, you take your life into your own hands. I'd suggest you conclude your business here, take your bruises, and leave while you still can." David slowly eased his way toward the back door.

"I'll make sure he vacates the property," Charlie said, a wicked smirk curling at the corners of her lips.

"It's nice to see you, Tim," Andrew said, clapping Tim on the shoulder and then smiling at his dad, who still hadn't relaxed enough to greet his unexpected guests. Max couldn't seem to take his eyes off me. I could see the respect and submission to my wolf in his eyes, not that I'd ever ask it of him. He was part of my family and I claimed them all as mine. Their submission was not required.

Laura threw her arms around me and hugged me close before taking a deep breath and moving to stand next to Max. "Please, won't everyone sit down? I have coffee on and I'm sure there's a lot to discuss, especially considering we just threw Stephon's guard dog out."

Tim laughed as Charlie walked through the door, grinning like a Cheshire cat. "He won't be back for a while. He's pretty much just been handed his dignity in a paper bag."

"Okay, kids, so besides inciting Stephon's bully, what are these new developments you wanted to discuss?" Tim smiled and took a chair at the table. Charlie continued to stand. She appeared to be constantly keeping watch, but she was trying not to be obvious about it.

"Well, Andrew and I are both getting stronger. The speed at which we can shift is becoming faster. We both took our third shape today and it was painless and fast. The amount of time we needed to remain in the new form was only a couple hours at most."

"It does sound like you are coming into your pureblood abilities rather quickly. Don't rush things, Lance." Tim frowned a bit. "You're really new to this."

"I know, but I feel like we should both be able to change into anything we want, any time we want, without pain or stress. This last time, with the polar bear, it was like I thought about being a bear and then I was the bear, effortlessly." I struggled to explain something I barely had a handle on myself as I took the seat Laura had previously occupied.

"And Lance cut my mental ties to Stephon, and I do mean cut. I haven't felt anything from him for hours." Andrew stood beside me. "Stephon's always been there. I can't remember a time when he wasn't a part of me. We're all mentally bound to our benefactors, some of us more strongly than others. Stephon has always prized this family—myself especially."

"You're all bound to Stephon like that? Having him in your mind, giving you pain if he doesn't like what you're doing?" It was more of a rhetorical question, because I already knew the answer. That vampire controlled my family, but they belonged to me.

"Yes, dear. He's having fits in all of our heads right now. We're all struggling to keep him at bay, but we won't be able to keep it up for long," Laura replied, cringing under the strain, leaning into Max's embrace.

"May I? I'd like to try something, if you don't mind."

"Oh, you think so?" Andrew asked me, picking up my train of thought.

"Yes, I know what to look for, and he's really pissed me off. I'd like to show him just how much. Besides, you are *my* family." I stood up and approached Jack first.

"What's he going to do?" Jack nervously looked from Andrew to me.

"Wouldn't you like a little privacy from that Peeping-Tom vampire?" I asked Jack, smiling down at him. Jack laughed and relaxed as I placed a hand on each of his shoulders and let my wolf loose, allowing my mind to sink into Jack's. My wolf liked the twins. He affectionately greeted Jack's wolf and then began searching for the touch of the vampire that tortured Jack's cub. My wolf snarled—this would stop now. We knew what we were hunting and found the mental tether almost immediately. Jack's wolf cringed, trying to get away from the screaming vampire in the back of his mind, like a dog straining at a leash. A growl began to rumble in my throat, low at first. My wolf snapped at the vampire, who drew back, not expecting another wolf in the cub's mind. When he flinched away, I struck, severing the connection between the two. And then Jack was free. I felt him sigh with relief as Stephon disappeared from his mind and I slipped from his thoughts. Jack leaned forward, a look of blissful relief on his face as he put his head on the cool surface of the table.

"You okay?" I hoped I hadn't hurt him in the process.

"It's the first quiet moment I've gotten all day. I'm fine… better than fine. Thank you." Jack grinned, but left his head resting on the table.

I moved on to Joe, freeing him with the same process. Max held Angela sleeping in his arms. Her link could hardly be thought of as a tether. Stephon obviously hadn't turned his rage on her. The vamp at least showed a minimum of scruples. She was so young, the vampire hadn't become a major part of her mind or world. So severing the unused connection didn't even disturb the sleeping child.

Laura proved a little more difficult since her wolf kept getting in my way, trying to get between me and the vampire's mind. In her mind, I could see she thought of me as one of her cubs, and she wanted to protect me from his onslaught. I snarled as I worked to free Laura from him. The fury came down through the connections in waves, and I felt it growing as I removed him from the minds of each member of my family. I could hear him calling me a thief, leveling threats against my life for coming between him and *what* he considered his. That was where he was mistaken—my family was *not* property and would no longer be treated as such.

Andrew and Tim had to restrain Max as he sat back from the table. He shook violently, Stephon's grip on his mind overwhelming him as the vampire sought to maintain the connection and not allow me to break Max free. I touched his shoulder and slid into Max's mind. Stephon screamed, trying to force me out by his will alone. Max's wolf snarled at my intrusion, but he didn't try to stop me. I attacked the vampire's mind full on. The battle took but a few seconds. I could feel Stephon weakening—as far away as he was, and after feeling the backlash of having his connections cut from the rest of the family, he was exhausted. He didn't have the power to deny my wolf.

Stay away from my family. They're mine. They don't need you interfering in their lives anymore. They're perfectly capable of taking care of themselves. If you need to contact them, try a damn phone. If they don't want to talk to you, they won't answer.

Who do you belong to? Who's threatening my wolves? Stephon snarled. *You may cut them from me mentally, but they're still mine to look after.*

I belong to no one. Haven't you figured it out yet? Surely you've seen everything Andrew's lived through and what he knows, having been connected to his mind. Tim has sent you the test results. You know exactly who I am. I heard Andrew chuckle in the back of my mind.

What are you after? Stephon seemed to hesitate, as if he was considering I might be telling the truth.

That's not something we need to discuss right now. We're stressing poor Max enough as it is. Andrew and I can come to you or you can come to us. Either way, I suggest we meet. If you intend to come to the ranch, it's considered polite to call first— using a phone. I cut the connection before Stephon could reply.

Andrew's belly laughter practically shook the pictures from the walls. He stood there, wiping tears from his face. "I could almost see the look on his face. Oh, you pissed him off big-time, love." Andrew roared with laughter, unable to contain himself. Chagrined, I glanced around the table at my now free family.

Max was bent over the table, holding his head, but it was with a look of complete relief. "Thank you so much. Having my family free from him—at least in this way—is worth any headache."

"You're more than welcome. You are my family."

"What did he do in the end? I could feel his fury, but I couldn't concentrate enough to understand what was being said," Max asked, somewhat distracted by Andrew's laughter.

"I told him to leave my family alone, and that Andrew and I would be coming for a visit. Or if he preferred, he could come here, but that it was polite to call ahead first," I said, a little sheepishly.

"He told Stephon to use a phone." Laughter rolled around the table, slowly subsiding, then beginning again as the phone rang. I could hear the hissing, angry voice as Andrew answered the phone.

"Why, hello, Stephon, so nice to hear from you. I'm guessing you're calling because you're upset with my mate. Sorry, Stephon, but he's totally wild and free. He does what he wants to and he can be hard to control from time to time."

Explain! I want to know why I'm defending my mind and my wolves from some man claiming to be your mate. I thought he was killing you. I first lost you and then the family. You have no idea how badly you scared me. Then, as I'm desperately trying to hold on to Max, I've got him attacking me and telling me to leave his family alone.

"He's very strong-willed and rather opinionated. As you can tell, he's also very talented." The yelling seemed to reduce in volume until it was but a snarl.

I don't give a damn. I'm your benefactor. How can I protect you if I have no idea what's really going on!

"Nothing's really changed, Stephon. We're still your beneficiaries. Still under your control, the only difference is you can't access our minds whenever you want." Andrew began to shake his head.

Goddammit, Andrew. What am I supposed to do now? You know the council would never approve of any of your people being without guidance. I have to get the mental bindings back in place before they discover your release.

"I wouldn't recommend that."

Look, if he's your mate and you intend to keep him, then ultimately I'll have to bind him to me, whether he likes it or not. He can stay and become one of my beneficiaries.

"I think if you attempt to bind him to you, you'll probably end up with much more than just a headache." Andrew rolled his eyes and sighed.

You know I don't have a choice in this. The council demands all shifters have a beneficiary and be bound for everyone's protection.

"Suit yourself. Oh, Tim would like to talk to you." Tim had been laughing at the exchange and had motioned for Andrew to hand over the phone.

"Hello, Stephon. I just wanted to let you know I've spoken with my father, Lord Basil. He's very interested in meeting Lance. I believe he thinks of him as a grandson," Tim chatted amicably, the conversation having suddenly become one-sided.

"Yes. Well, actually, his name is Prince Marcus Lance Fenrir Fitz, as you well know since you've had the paperwork for a couple of days now. I'm sure you're familiar with the family names involved." I could only imagine what Stephon was saying to Tim.

"No, my father does *not* wish to add Lance to—" Tim paused as Stephon interrupted him.

"Of course not. If he was interested in—" Tim sighed as he tried to get a word in edgewise.

"Yes, he is of the royal line, and a pureblood of the rarest of bloodlines." Tim smiled at whatever Stephon said.

"Yes, I see you understand. I *am* his vassal, as are a few others, and we take our duty very seriously. I'm sure you wouldn't have us do any less." Tim nodded as whatever Stephon said amused him.

"Sorry you feel that way, Stephon. Now, are you accusing me of theft? Theft of a person? That would be kidnapping, you know? Those are some very serious charges, Stephon. Especially since the shape-shifters are only under our care—we don't technically own them. Because, as everyone knows, slavery is wrong—isn't that right, Stephon?" The yelling I could hear from the phone would've been deafening if the speaker on the cell weren't so limited as to the amount of sound it could transfer.

"I figured you'd see it my way. See you soon." Tim was enjoying himself way too much, a grin spreading across his face as he hung up the phone.

"Thank you, Tim." I nodded to the doctor. He continued to surprise me, and I admired his fortitude for standing up to a born vampire.

"Okay, we don't have a lot of time to plan now. I'm pretty sure he'll be here in a day or two—unless he sends an armed escort to bring you to him, which would actually make more sense. He has more control of you that way. What is your ultimate goal where Stephon's concerned?" Tim asked.

"I want Andrew and my family to be free, but I won't take the choice away from them, it has to be what they want. To be honest, beyond freeing Andrew, I'm not sure exactly what I should be doing. I don't know what's best. I didn't grow up in this world. Hell, I barely know my own people and suddenly I'm a prince. Seeing Andrew's memories and feeling how he felt growing up, makes me a little more comfortable. It helps me to know myself and my people better, but there's still so much I don't know. Each day I'm learning more about myself and this world." I looked at Laura, Max, my little brothers Jake and Joe, Angela, and Andrew—*my* Andrew. "Maybe instead of asking me what I want to do, I should be asking all of you—what do you want from me?"

"Love, you know my answer. I've always craved freedom. You know my thoughts as well as you know your own." Andrew pressed his chest against my back, hugging me tightly to him.

I looked to Max.

"Freedom's a fine thing as a concept, but I have a family to care for. This land is ours and it can't be taken from us, but if we're freed, we lose our pack. I don't think we should cut that connection just yet. Sandy's the head of our family, but she has a different benefactor than we do. Cutting us from Stephon would effectively remove us from our pack. We'd become ostracized because the other benefactors would prevent the rest of our family from contacting us. There are many benefactors who are much worse than Stephon. He's been good to our family." Max walked around behind Laura and reached for her hand. She nodded to him and smiled sadly. "Andrew's desired his freedom all his life. We understand his need to be free. Freedom's something I've always wanted, to be able to choose for myself, not that I regret one moment of my life." He gazed down into Laura's eyes. "I think the best choice for my family right now is for you to free Andrew, and the rest of us will be free when we all are free."

"Besides, the fewer demands you place on Stephon, the more likely he is to agree and allow you to go free. He isn't unreasonable, and he truly cares." Laura eyed Andrew. "He's done a lot for you and he doesn't deserve to be treated like the enemy. Aristocratic… yes. Overly dramatic… sometimes. But evil? No. You, more than any of us, know he's not evil, Andrew. You need to remember that."

My man took a deep breath and nodded in agreement with his mother. Even after all the pain, they still didn't see the vamp as the bad guy. Whatever his brainwashing technique, it seeded deep loyalty into their psyches. I'd have to try to keep my thoughts on the subject to myself.

"Do you think we should tell Sandy what we're up to? I really like her and I think she has a lot to offer." I grinned mischievously at Max.

"You know, you may have a point there. As matriarch, she does have some very interesting connections amongst the families. I'll call her. I'm sure she'd be willing to come by and see you again. She seemed very smitten with you." Max beamed at the idea of having the matriarch visit again.

CHAPTER 6

THE excitement over, my family began to relax, with fresh drinks for some of us and sighs of relief as the tension in the room eased from others. We retook our seats around the table. I was still quite tense, but Andrew's sigh of relief and his head against my shoulder had me smiling along with everyone else.

"You know, it was almost three hundred years ago… right after the Great War, when the treaty between the shifters and vampires had just been signed. I'd returned home when the fighting was done, and Lord Basil accepted me back as his personal secretary." Tim nodded for a moment, deep in thought. "If I remember correctly, Stephon was so against the beneficiary program that he refused to take on the shifters assigned to him, so he was brought up on charges before the Vampire Council. Even in those days, Lord Basil sat on the council. He was against the beneficiary program too, but he was in the minority. As his secretary, I was allowed in the council room to take notes."

"Stephon didn't want to be a benefactor?" I frowned, unable to picture the highly possessive born vampire that I loved to hate as a rebel, going against his own government.

"As I remember, it was 1726…," Tim began, recounting past events in such great detail, we could almost see them.

Stephon glanced around the courtroom. The heat and humidity were stifling. Since the war, the council had taken to having all sessions behind closed doors, and this time was no exception, regardless of the fact that they were situated in the tropics and it was the middle of summer. It made no difference. The council seemed to enjoy tormenting their own people as much as they did the shifters.

"Lord Stephon La'Fayette."

Stephon rose from his seat in the gallery upon being thus addressed. "Yes, Grand Master." He nodded to the leader of the council of seven.

"Please take the stand before the council."

"As you wish, Grand Master." Stephon stepped from his seat in the gallery. As he went down the stairs, he was met partway by an escort of warriors, the guardians of the council. Just a short time ago the guardians would've been protecting his person, not seeing him as a possible threat to the safety of the council. Stephon took his place in the speaker's box, facing some of his biggest foes as well as his friends. Little had changed since he'd stepped down from the council, when they'd decided to go to war.

"Stephon, what are you doing? You, better than most, know the consequences for refusing a mandate from this council." The Grand Master frowned. "You've been ordered to take over as benefactor to a number of shifter families, as have all born vampires. It is our responsibility to prevent a war from ever happening again. In order to ensure the safety of our race, this council has determined that careful monitoring and controlled breeding of the shifters will safeguard that future. Never again

can they have the power to threaten the secrecy of our society, our existence, or their own."

"So that's what you tell yourself in order to sleep at night?" Stephon sadly shook his head. "I wondered how you justified such slavery. You're talking about shifters as if they're prized breeding animals. These are sentient beings, not so very different from us. They were our allies in the Blood Wars. If the veil falls and we're once again faced with the prospect of Seelie and Unseelie forces invading this plane, without the full strength of our allies, we will die just as surely."

"We've not seen the fair folk for more than a century. The council has determined the shifters are a greater, more immediate threat. There has never been an instance of the barrier's failure since it was erected, therefore there is no reason to believe it will happen in the future." The Grand Master held up a hand, silencing further debate. "This is all beside the point. These decisions have already been made and are not the reason you stand before us."

"I will not treat the children and families of honored friends and warriors as livestock. What you are doing is beneath you. You're supposed to be the moral backbone of our race, and yet you believe this is the proper way to treat a great people and an honorable ally?" Stephon pointed to the shifters, lined up against the wall in chains.

"Careful, Lord Stephon La' Fayette. Your words border on treason against your race," the Grand Master snarled. "If you will not take on the shifters as beneficiaries, then the beings assigned to you will be executed. You'll be allowed to watch their deaths before you yourself are put to death for treason. Is that truly the road you wish to take?"

Stephon shook his head, gripping the banister in front of him, hissing his frustration. He turned to look at the shifters.

There were some men, who were clearly soldiers, and women, tightly clutching their children. An infant bawled in the arms of a young girl who couldn't have been more than twelve. Altogether, there were some fifteen people whose lives would be forfeit if he refused to abide by the council's rules.

"What time frame are you proposing? We take on the families and care for them as if they were drones. But even drones are released on good behavior after a few decades. What of these?" Stephon motioned to the people cowering against the wall.

"The peace treaty their leaders signed gave us complete control of their race for the rest of time. We've determined there are too few of them left to maintain a viable breeding pool. We've had to separate some committed pairs. They shall be bred with humans in order to keep their race alive." A cold smile crossed the Grand Master's face as he glared at the shifters as though they were no more than filth beneath his feet. Stephon searched the faces of the few remaining friends he had on the council; most appeared too ashamed to meet his eyes. Only one, Lord Basil, met his gaze, albeit with sadness and regret.

Stephon closed his eyes and pinched the bridge of his nose in frustration. There was no winning this fight, at least not in front of the council. Maybe he and his friends could maneuver behind the scenes to prevent the mutation of the shifter people.

"I watched the man bow to the demands of the vampire council. When the meeting ended, his first concern was for the people he'd taken into his care and getting them out of the council chambers. In time, he took his people to the new world, putting as much distance as he could between himself and the council. He reunited as many of the families as he could, but his actions were monitored. He was forced to breed humans with the shifters. Even in the new world, he couldn't get far enough away from the council to prevent that." Tim met my eyes, his true age suddenly apparent in the weary expression that had settled upon his face.

"Well, that's reassuring—assuming he still feels the same way." I sighed and tried to focus. "Okay, one problem at a time. So Stephon isn't really a bad guy, even though I don't like him much. Maybe I'll feel differently when I meet him, although I feel like I've known him forever, through Andrew." I leaned back against Andrew, and he massaged my shoulders, trying to help relieve me of some of the tension.

"He'd be a good ally to have," Tim stressed, knowing as they all did, how reluctant I was to accept the vampire. "Maybe he'd even know of other born vampires, like him, who are secretly working to help shifters. It'd be a good beginning. Through his dealings with other benefactors, he'll know which families are strong and which families have been decimated."

"I wouldn't count on the royal family knowing the true condition of anyone," Max rubbed at his temples. "From what Sandy tells me, they've been reduced to barely more than human and they're too caught up in their own self-importance. Most don't live past a hundred years. Still, they *are* the 'royal family,' and they do make most of the major decisions, even though most of them have no education whatsoever." Max ran a hand through his hair. His body still trembled uncontrollably, the remains of the mental battle still affecting him.

Tim shook his head in disgust. "Charlie, what do you think would be the best approach to Stephon?"

"Stephon? That's easy. I think a mixture of power, threats, and charm will win him over. He won't respect you unless you can show him you're more powerful than he is. He won't give Andrew over to you without being threatened and forced into it. He'll see it as his duty to protect him, even from you, if he feels you're not powerful enough to do the job. I also think he has a soft spot for Andrew." Charlie chuckled and gave Tim a knowing look. "If you can, charm him and flatter him. Tell him how well he's done his duty. Compliment his intelligence, and maybe even flatter him about how wise he must be for having been around so long…. Ugh." Charlie made a face. "If you do all that, he'll probably be putty in your hands."

Everyone around the table laughed at Charlie's disgust. She obviously preferred a much more straightforward approach, as did I. *I'm going to need some coaching on this whole flattery and charm thing.* Andrew snorted inside my head, and I rolled my eyes.

"Okay, so what should I expect? Will he try to attack me physically? Will he attack Andrew, try to use him against me so I'll give up? What?" I asked with exasperation.

"Oh, God, no. I wouldn't expect anything like that. He's very intellectual and not a fighter at all. He doesn't see you as a threat. He hasn't seen a real pureblood in centuries. He won't accept our assessment of you—we're just drones, after all. He'll need to see you for himself. You'll have to demonstrate your power and, in the process, sufficiently threaten him in order to get his full attention." Charlie wagged a finger at me. "Don't underestimate him. His appearance and the initial impression he gives are very… deceiving. He abhors violence. He's seen enough wars in his time that he won't want any blood spilled in his home." Charlie's wicked sneer would've scared the crap out of me if I hadn't known she was on our side. "We'll be there, of course, as your vassals, and that'll just annoy him. I need to pull together a couple more warriors to make up a full formal guard. Even though you won't really need the help, the man lives for a good show, so we'll give him one."

"Okay, I think we should get Sandy's take on this tomorrow," Max said. "I'd like to know what to expect from the royal family once the vampires are made aware of Lance's existence. We definitely need to get them on our side—even if they are a useless bunch of pups." Max grabbed his phone. "Hopefully, Sandy will know which families are still viable and which are in dire straits."

"Where do we go from here? I mean, if we get Stephon on our side, and we get the royals on our side as well as the matriarchs... what's next?" I asked, bewildered.

"Then we'd need to formally petition the council for Right to Rule under the terms of the treaty. They'll have to agree to it because you fulfill their requirements, but they'll make things as difficult and mired in political posturing as they possibly can. At any rate, I don't think we need to worry about it right now. Let's just concentrate on getting Andrew free. If we can't free Andrew, things could get complicated." Tim's voice was soft, filled with regret. "I'd also expect to receive more death threats as your presence becomes more known."

"I agree. We need to focus, take this one step at a time." Andrew rubbed my arms. I knew he could feel my spirits falling as I thought of all the pain my mother had caused, all because she'd loved the wrong man.

"Okay, kids, I think we've accomplished all we can today. Charlie and I need to get back and start making some phone calls so we can finish gathering your guard." Tim stood, getting ready to leave.

"I have a few in mind, specifically." Charlie's twisted smile once again sent a shiver down my spine. I was beginning to think she did it deliberately, getting a perverse kind of kick knowing the effect it had on those who saw it. The others rose and followed them out while Andrew and I hung back in the kitchen.

I could hear Charlie and Tim saying their good-nights to the family as they left. Despite Charlie's appearance, I really liked her. She hid nothing—if she thought it, she said it. No subterfuge. No games. No lies. You knew instantly where you stood with her. Andrew felt my fondness for both Tim and Charlie as we watched them go.

He took a seat and pulled me onto his lap. "We're going to be fine, love. Whatever comes, we'll handle it together."

"I know. I just feel overwhelmed," I whispered. I could put on a good, strong front for the others and sarcasm was my best friend, but Andrew knew exactly how insignificant and lost I felt. They all were counting on me, and I didn't know if I could measure up. How could I—a runaway street kid with no education—free these people? I wasn't exceptional; I was just me. I felt and heard Andrew's denial of those thoughts as he kissed my neck and hugged me tight.

The family came back in, having said good-bye to the vampires.

"Sandy agreed to come. She'll be here first thing in the morning. I told her a little of what we discussed, and she has some ideas of her own as well."

Fatigue was beginning to set in, and I let out a sigh. Andrew could feel my tension and my desire for a hasty retreat. I just wanted to go back to our cottage. I needed to feel safe. I needed him. He smiled at me and placed a hand at the back of my neck, rubbing gently. I could feel his agreement, his own need to go home. Things were all starting to jumble in my mind, and I had to get it sorted out, prepare myself for the reality of what we were going to try to do. We really were going to attempt to free his people—a shifter revolution.

"It seems like everything's going to happen in the morning. I think Lance and I are going to return to the cottage. It's getting late, and we still cherish our alone time." His teasing grin had me blushing with embarrassment. I stood, growling softly as I hit him

84

on the arm. *That wasn't quite how I wanted to make our polite escape,* I told him, as I took his hand and pulled him to his feet. Everyone laughed as we headed for the door.

After saying good night to my family, Andrew led me toward the barn. He wanted to have a vehicle at the cottage. We walked through the large open doors to his black Dodge Ram 2500 truck. Being four-wheel drive, it could handle just about any terrain with ease. Andrew beamed with pride as he caressed the hood after removing the protective tarp. Once we had both climbed in, he turned the key and started the truck. He loved the roar and power of the engine. The truck purred as Andrew backed out of the barn, then roared as he gunned the gas, speeding off toward the cottage. The truck made short work of the gravel road, and before I knew it, we were pulling up our drive.

I'd grown to love spending time with Andrew's family, but having a place all to ourselves really couldn't be beat. Although I had gotten better around other people, I still preferred being alone with Andrew in our little home. I could tell he missed the intimate contact with his family, but he too craved solitude, time for just us.

As we approached our little clearing, I could hear the clang of metal striking metal over the noise from the truck engine. Andrew hit the gas, charging forward. Charlie stood in the center of the clearing, three drones around her. Even severely outnumbered, she kept them at bay, but I could see she couldn't hold out much longer. Andrew barreled the truck right into the middle of the fight. Charlie leapt at the last second, landing upright on the hood of the truck.

I didn't know what she was doing here, but she needed help. I opened the door and began to shift. I wanted lethal and I wanted power. Even before my feet hit the ground, I'd become a white tiger, my clothing falling in shredded tatters around me. Andrew caught sight of my choice as we both rounded the front of the vehicle. I saw he'd become a polar bear. Charlie crouched on one knee on the hood of the truck as we attacked her aggressors from both sides. Our combined roars echoed over the clearing and could probably be heard at the ranch. Charlie didn't move. We could see the shock in the eyes of the attacking vampires as we approached, one from either side of the truck. I chanced a glance at Charlie; she panted heavily, pain and exhaustion reflected in her movements. As we closed in on the three vampires, I snarled and lunged at the vampire on the right while Andrew took the one on the left. It was no contest. We dispatched the vampires on either side in seconds, completely tearing them apart. The third, having been injured by Charlie, sought escape by darting around the truck and then running with lightning speed down the road. It was his misfortune to be met by a pair of sandy-coated wolves. The twins had apparently heard our battle roars and come running to our aid. The slight hesitation in the vampire's escape gave Andrew the moment's time he needed to catch the vampire with a huge paw and part his head from his shoulders, black blood oozing into the ground as the body collapsed in front of him.

With the threat gone, Charlie collapsed. She twitched uncontrollably, her body wracked with seizure like spasms, as she lay across the hood of the truck. I leaned against the vehicle in concern, despite the fact that my two huge front paws were sure to leave claw marks in the paint, chuffing softly. *If I licked her wounds, would it help her or harm her?* I didn't want to take the chance. I looked to Andrew, who had returned to human form and stood beside me.

"Jack, Joe, check the forest and the surrounding area. Make sure there aren't more of them hiding out there," Andrew bellowed, and the twins took off running for the trees.

She's hurt really bad. I don't think we have time to wait for the twins. Charlie was losing blood and the convulsive twitching hadn't stopped. We needed to get her to Tim—and fast. I didn't know what to do to help her. I transformed and pulled her into my arms, then applied pressure to some of the open wounds. Either she weighed much less than I'd expected or the adrenaline pumping through my veins had made me much stronger. She felt fragile in my arms.

Andrew helped me up into the cab of the truck, and I clutched her tightly in my lap, her head against my shoulder. Then he joined me, taking the driver's seat. With a twist of the wheel and a stomp on the gas pedal, Andrew spun the still-running truck around and headed in the direction of the farm. Charlie's labored breathing and shaking continued. She had moments of seeming consciousness, but then her eyes would just roll back in her head. I talked softly to her, trying to reassure her. Driving wildly, Andrew poured every ounce of the truck's substantial power into speeding, sending a plume of gravel into the air trailing our progress down the dirt road.

"OnStar… call Dr. Tim Carlson."

The sound of the ringing phone did little to assuage the panic I felt over Charlie's ever-weakening condition. All I could do was hope we made it to Tim in time for him to help her—*if* he could help her.

"Dr. Carlson."

"Tim, it's Andrew. We found Charlie in the meadow fighting three drones. We killed them, but not before she suffered some serious injuries. I think we're dealing with poisoned weapons here." Andrew sped past the ranch and out onto the pavement. I felt the truck surge forward as he pushed the engine to the limit, barreling down the highway.

"What are her symptoms?"

"She's bleeding pretty badly and convulsing. She seems to be slipping in and out of consciousness. Her skin is hot to the touch as well," I told Tim, as our conversation spilled through the truck's speakers, through the magic of OnStar.

"Get her here as soon as possible. I've got blood we can give her, but if it's poison, it all depends on the level of exposure. There may be nothing we can do. In the meantime, keep talking to her and try to keep her calm and awake. Just get here soon."

The drive felt like we were going in slow motion, even though I knew Andrew was breaking every speed limit along the way. The whole time, I spoke softly to Charlie and gently stroked her face, asking her to stay with me.

"You hear me, girl? You're not going anywhere. You have a job to do, and I intend to see you do it." She locked her gaze on me as I alternated between promises and threats—anything to keep her focused on me, on my eyes. The wounds covering her body were ugly—gaping, bleeding gashes that oozed a black viscous fluid. I could tell she was in excruciating pain. Her mind was slipping into survival mode—fight or flight. I could tell she wanted to attack me and yet she struggled to prevent it, knowing I wasn't the one that hurt her. Conscious thought wasn't going to last much longer. She needed blood. I was willing to give her what she needed, but I had no idea what shifter blood would do to her. My wolf didn't think my blood would help her.

I kept talking to her, calmly holding her gaze. The sound of the squealing breaks actually reached me before the sudden jarring as the truck swerved around a corner. I braced myself against the dashboard to prevent us from becoming hood ornaments. Andrew slammed on the brakes again as we came to an abrupt stop. We'd arrived at the back of the clinic, in a partially hidden alleyway. Tim stood, waiting for us. As the truck slid to a halt, he opened the door and grabbed Charlie from my arms, rushing with her into the clinic almost before the truck had fully stopped. Andrew leapt out the driver's door and slammed it behind him. I met him by the hood, both of us running after Tim.

It didn't dawn on me until after we'd entered the clinic that Andrew and I were standing there completely nude as Tim worked on Charlie. The thought was a passing one, overridden by other considerations, such as Charlie's worsening condition. She'd gone still. I couldn't even be sure she was still breathing.

Tim's gaze never stopped moving over her, assessing her injuries as he grabbed bags of human blood and hung them from an IV pole. "I'm sorry if this offends you, but it's the best way to do it."

"Don't worry about me, Tim. Just help her," I nearly screamed at him.

He sliced open a corner of the bag of blood and forced it between Charlie's lips. She instantly gasped, as though someone had handed her a lifeline. She began taking great gulps, swallowing as quickly as she could, but her eyes remained unfocused and unseeing. Tim motioned to Andrew. He took over feeding Charlie as Tim began to examine her wounds. They oozed black pus and the stench was almost overpowering.

"She's been poisoned. The blades must have been treated. I don't know if the blood will do more than keep her here. As far as I know, there isn't an antidote for this." Tim wiped the black ooze from the wounds, trying to clean them, but they continued to fester, the infection spreading faster than he could clean.

"Tim, when Jack was hurt the first time we fought drones, my saliva cleansed the wound and healed him. Granted, the wound oozed yellow, not black, but my saliva worked like an antidote. Do you think it could help Charlie and clean the poison out?" I asked. The wounds continued to get more and more septic, even as he furiously worked, moving his hands faster than I could track.

"I need more blood here. She's already finished this one," Andrew said.

Tim handed Andrew another liter of blood. Andrew took the bag, cut the end open and poured it into Charlie's mouth. Tim was right—the blood wasn't healing her, simply sustaining her.

"It's possible, but vampires and shifters have very different physiologies and very different methods of healing. It may be that what's cleansing and healing for you could kill or harm us. On the other hand, nothing we're doing here is helping her. I'm ready to try anything. I say if you're willing, give it a try. Even if you aren't able to do anything but clean the wounds of the poison, the blood should be able to heal the rest." Tim looked in my eyes.

There was no question of my willingness. I liked Charlie and I didn't want to lose one of my own when I was just getting used to having people around I felt I could trust. I shifted to the wolf and stood on my back legs with my front paws on the table. My wolf sniffed at Charlie. She had the distinct scent of a vampire, like old blood, but she belonged to me. The stench of rot from her poisoned wounds gagged me, causing the wolf to curl his lips at the vile smell of the black ooze. I felt saliva flowing in my mouth. I cringed, not knowing what was coming. Would the saliva heal, like it had Jack, or would it make matters worse and burn her like acid as it had the other drones I'd bitten?

Please let me help her and not hurt her. I swept my tongue across one of the smaller oozing cuts on Charlie's arm. It tasted of rotted flesh and old dead blood. I tried to spit the black ooze out of my mouth onto the floor, but it ended up more as gagging. I shook my head and raked my tongue against my front teeth, which just seemed to make the taste worse. I ignored everything except working on cleaning the wound. I could feel the poison sinking into my body just from this little contact alone. My stomach clenched, wanting to heave. I watched as the wound I'd laved began to knit and heal over.

"It's working, Lance. Keep going." I'd started with a small wound, to test my saliva. This time Tim pointed to a much more severe wound on Charlie's thigh. The cut had gone straight to the bone. I worked steadily from then on, cleaning the wounds and then retching out the ooze. By the time I'd finished the last wound, I felt truly sick. There was no way to be sure if the problem was the pus or the vampire blood. Nauseous and dizzy, I wavered on my feet. I didn't want to pass out on Andrew again, but I could feel the darkness reaching for me.

Andrew had the same concentration on his face as I had, my determination spilling over into him. He'd become so absorbed in getting fresh blood into Charlie and watching her eyes and reactions, he missed how sick I'd become. I could vaguely hear him shouting to Tim as things went black and I crumpled to the floor.

CHAPTER 7

I COULD hear the insistent beep of a nearby machine—it was annoying. I could also hear Andrew calling for Tim. The panic in him spilled through our link, and I could feel it. Damn, I wasn't going to pass out on him anymore. *Please, love, I'm here. Just… can you please stop shouting at Tim? I feel like I've got the world's worst hangover.*

Andrew held my hand, squeezing it gently. *Please, leannan, can you open your eyes?*

I dreaded opening them because of the pounding in my head, but I knew it would ease his stress if I could make myself do it. *Just give me a minute.* Even mentally, drawing the words together took effort.

Tim whispered—it was his voice, only at the same time it resembled a mountain slide of boulders as it echoed against the pain in my head. "Yes, he's conscious. Oh, what a relief. Lance, child, can you please open your eyes for us? I need to determine if there is any neurological damage. I need to try and help you heal."

Slowly, I opened my eyes, letting out a soft moan. The light hurt, but not as badly as I'd feared. With each passing moment, the pain lessened. My stomach felt a bit queasy, but again, much better than when I passed out.

"Oh, my love… you scared me—again." The scent of Andrew's fear, palpable in the room, washed over me. I looked deeply into his eyes.

"Well, at least it looks like you let Tim keep his arms this time," I teased, taking a deep breath as the pain receded further.

"You gave us all a real scare. You had a reaction to the poison. Didn't you feel it coming on?" Tim asked softly.

"Well, yeah, but I had to keep going, couldn't stop. It was working and I had to finish healing Charlie." I felt a little nauseous, remembering the black ooze.

I heard a low, menacing growl in the background. I clung to Andrew's arm—the sound wasn't coming from him. I glanced around the room, but saw nothing that appeared threatening. "Is Charlie okay?" I searched Andrew's eyes for the answer.

"She'll be fine." The growling continued softly in the background. I struggled, pushing myself to sit. Andrew helped me upright as Tim disconnected the heartbeat monitor, then inspected my eyes.

"I believe the trouble has passed. Your body has overcome the poison, although it caused many of your systems to shut down in order to expel it and heal the damage. With Jack, you only had to deal with one wound, while Charlie had multiple wounds and you were exposed to much more of the toxin." Tim ran a hand through his hair, clearly upset by all of this. "You must remember something. *You* are our first priority, always. Anytime something makes you feel sick, you must tell us. I might have been able to help sooner if I'd known you were feeling ill."

"Sorry… I just got so wrapped up in being able to help. I didn't realize how bad I felt until things started spinning and I threw up. I didn't mean to scare anyone." I snuggled into Andrew's arms, and just the feel of our skin touching eased the stress on both of us. The growling continued somewhere behind Andrew. With a frown, I finally leaned around Andrew to see Charlie sitting up, leaning against the wall. She glowered angrily at me.

"Oh, Charlie, I'm so glad you're feeling better." Relief washed over me. I got to my feet somewhat unsteadily. Thank goodness, someone had given me a hospital gown. Andrew held my elbow to help me stay upright. I wobbled weakly at first, then found my balance and made my way over to sit beside her. I wrapped my arms around her and gave her a squeeze. Charlie rolled her eyes as she reluctantly returned my affection, but continued to growl her annoyance. She leaned back and forced me to look into her eyes.

"Let's get something straight, because you obviously don't understand the whole concept of vassals. We're here to help you. Your life is infinitely more important than mine. It's my job to protect *you* and die for *you*. You taking risks with your life to save mine is totally unacceptable. Do you understand me?"

I laughed and drew her tighter into my arms, even though the touch of vampire to shifter gave me goose bumps and made my skin crawl, a phenomenon Tim had demonstrated for me not so long ago when I was discovering myself and the differences between shifters and the rest of the world. To me, it proved she was alive. "I'm glad you're okay too." I completely ignored her eye roll. She shook her head, sighed exasperatedly, and began her growling anew. Tim and Andrew laughed softly and refused to meet her dirty looks.

Charlie had healed quickly once the poison had been removed. Her leather outfit needed some mending, and she had some vivid red scars on her chalk white skin, but we all were well. Somehow, we'd survived another attempt on my life.

"What happened, Charlie? Why were you at the cottage?" I asked. Now that I was feeling better, my curiosity was getting the better of me.

"When we left Andrew's parents' house, Tim decided to return to town. Since I renewed my vow, I began checking out the cabin on a regular basis—especially at night just to be sure you're safe." I scowled at the thought of her skulking around in those dark woods, alone at night. I had to hand it to her, though— neither Andrew nor I had scented her anywhere around the territory; the woman knew what she was doing. "When I reached the meadow, I knew immediately there were intruders. Their scent covered the place. They'd done nothing to mask their presence from other vampires. I'm not sure you'd have realized they were there lying in wait for you, but I felt them immediately."

"You can't keep doing this by yourself. I appreciate you wanting to keep us safe, but, Charlie, if we hadn't come along when we did, we wouldn't be having this conversation right now," I scolded her. "I won't have anyone dying for me— especially when there isn't anybody at the cottage to protect. You should have saved yourself and escaped to warn us. We could've gone back together and hunted the trespassers down. I would've been very unhappy if I'd returned to the meadow and discovered your body ripped to shreds." Tim nodded and walked out of the room, carrying out the garbage we'd created of his supplies.

"If you insist, I'll make sure to never travel alone—as long as you no longer travel without a guard. Someone will need to keep watch while you're at the cottage. I'm not too concerned about the safety of your family at this point, but whoever your enemy is, they know where you live. Luckily for us, they seem to be unaware of your increasing power. For now, you count on me to always be in the vicinity. I will do my best to be discreet, but I'll be there all the same. By tomorrow I shall have a partner, so I will no longer be working alone," Charlie stubbornly insisted.

"Do you really think that's necessary, Charlie?" I feared for her safety.

"Yes, I really do. The next attack won't be as impulsive. Someone has been steadily underestimating you, but they won't do so for much longer. If I can give you enough warning, you can defend yourself—with my help. We must be ready. The cottage is easily defendable, one road in and out. We'll have a guard there in no more than two days. From then on, I will be able to protect you properly." She kept an arm draped lightly around my shoulders and smiled at me. I knew then she'd grown fond of me, despite all the growling. "But until then, I'll guard you myself."

Tim wandered into the room and put away some supplies, then filled us in as he continued to clean up. "We called Andrew's parents. Max heard the roars and followed the twins to the cottage. He helped them make sure they'd destroyed the bodies of all three vampires. After that, they did a security sweep, but they didn't turn up anything. For the time being, the twins are staying at the cottage to make sure no one else trespasses. Max installed a large yard light at the entrance where the road splits away from the farm to go up to the cottage. If it's well lit, there's less of a chance of someone making it up to the cottage unseen."

"Here's a list of people I'd like you to contact for me. You should recognize some of them. Others are warriors I've met over the years who we should be able to recruit," Charlie instructed as she handed a list of contacts over to Tim.

Tim nodded as he read over the list of names. "I'll make the calls. Why don't all of you get out of here and try to get some rest? That means you too, Charlie."

"I will," Charlie groaned as Tim followed us out to the truck.

Andrew and I climbed in, then opened the windows so we could continue to talk.

"I'll meet you at the cabin. I need to go by my apartment and change… get properly armed, too." Charlie patted the door of the truck and swiftly disappeared into the night.

"She's going to meet up with us *after* going for clothes and weapons? If we're driving, how can she manage that when she's on foot?" I asked as I turned to Tim, giving him a confused look.

"Charlie's incredibly fast. Always has been. Sometimes I think she teleports, but I've yet to be able to prove it." At that, Tim waved to us and went back into the clinic.

Andrew and I drove home through the darkness. It had been a very long night and it wasn't quite over yet. Dawn had yet to break on the horizon and the sky was still an inky black. My entire body felt like I'd been run over by a Mack truck, and I suspect I dozed off for at least part of the trip because it wasn't long before we arrived at the ranch. Max stood guard on the road leading to the cottage. I had never seen his wolf up close. If I weren't part beast myself, I'd have missed the almost solid-black wolf at the edge of the road, standing in the shadows. He stepped out and barked a greeting. Andrew stopped the car and we both got out. I put my arms around Max's black wolf and hugged him.

"Thank you so much. There are no words to express how much I appreciate everything you're doing for me," I whispered into Andrew's father's lupine ear. His ears twitched and he whined a bit as he nuzzled my neck then thumped his son on the leg with his tail, pushing him back toward the truck. We got the message. We got back in and drove up to the cottage. Andrew parked off to the side and we both just sat in the quiet of the cab, not speaking. The peace that seemed to permeate the meadow settled in our bones. We were finally home. The twins were standing watch at opposite ends of the clearing. The remnants of a fire crackled in the fire pit. It was mostly coals now, but I imagined it had been quite the blaze. A hint of burnt sugar, tar, and diesel fuel hung in the air, wafting from the fire—there was no mistaking the scent of burned vampire remains.

When we got out of the truck, Charlie strode out from the darkness at the side of the clearing, downwind from the twins. Both brothers yipped with surprise and concern, running full tilt to join us, growling menacingly at Charlie as if she were an intruder. Andrew held up a hand to his brothers but still they came, shifting to human as they got closer, completely unconcerned at being naked in front of a female.

"Where'd she come from?" Jack asked, staring at Charlie.

Charlie grinned, obviously pleased with herself at being able to get past the two young wolves. "I'm much faster than your average deer or rabbit. You never even saw or smelled me pass by."

"That's a neat trick. Can you teach me to do it?" asked Joe. He flashed her a grin. Charlie just shook her head.

"This is not the time for playing around, pup." Charlie looked at the two young wolves who'd been standing guard and frowned slightly. I couldn't be sure if she was upset because they saw her or if she thought they should've seen her sooner.

"I've checked the perimeter and spoken with Max. You're safe; nobody's been in or out since the attack." Charlie's gaze briefly met mine then returned to scanning for possible intruders.

"That's a relief." Andrew rubbed the small of my back. "Boys, why don't you go on home and get some rest? Tomorrow's already here, and I'm sure Dad's going to need help with chores."

"Yeah, I guess. We'll howl if anyone turns up on the road." Jack shuffled his feet, giving his twin brother a push, then turned back to Andrew. With a growl, Andrew enforced his order and they finally headed down the road, back toward the farm. Charlie smiled more warmly after the two young wolves than I'd thought her capable of. Almost immediately, her hard mask returned. She might have been a warrior, but I thought Charlie missed being around young ones. Well, she'd get her chance to see them again hanging around here. The twins were usually close at hand.

"Tim called me a few minutes ago and let me know the first of the guard will be here by morning, but until then I'll keep watch along with Max at the head of the road."

"Don't you need rest, Charlie?" I asked her, concerned. The woman had almost died earlier, and I didn't want to lose my friend.

She laughed at me "You worry too much, Lance. No, I don't need rest. Drones don't really sleep. We slow down a bit during the day, but I never really sleep. I'm fine. I'm not expecting any more trouble tonight. I'll just keep watch, more for my own peace of mind than anything else. Go to sleep. You're safe." Silently, Charlie jogged off into the woods and disappeared.

Andrew and I went into our cottage. The fires had burned low in the grates, but the coals were still sending out delicious warmth. Andrew added wood to both, to keep the fires going through what was left of the night. Bone-numbing exhaustion had my body feeling like lead, but my mind continued to circle the issues everyone had talked about before the attack. Andrew put on some water for chamomile tea. My man knew how to relax me. I walked over to the stereo and found some soft music, then curled up on the love seat, listening to the soft jazz riffs.

Andrew joined me, handed me a cup of tea, then slid in behind me. I sipped at the hot liquid and all the stress of the day washed from my mind as I rested my head against Andrew's chest, listening to his steady heartbeat. I could feel the love-filled thoughts that flowed through Andrew's mind as he slid his fingers through my hair. His contentment wrapped around me like a thick, warm blanket, separating me from the rest of the world. The heat of his chest against my back sank in to relieve the last tendrils of stress from my body. He surrounded me like a protective cocoon, absorbing me into himself. My mind began to slide completely into his, the two slowly becoming one. It was difficult to tell where Andrew ended and I began. There was no separation between us. In this moment, we were entirely one.

"I love you," I whispered and turned my face to Andrew, longing for him to capture my lips in a passionate kiss. I could feel his hunger and the need he tried to subdue lurking beneath his overwhelming love for me. "Don't hide how you feel. I want you too."

"Lance…," Andrew whispered. He swept my hair to the side and nipped at my neck. I moaned softly and leaned back as Andrew began to move his hands across my body, then let out a long, pleasure-filled sigh. I took his hand, rose, and led Andrew into the bedroom. I wanted to feel him inside me, to be joined in body as well as mind.

CHAPTER 8

I AWOKE snuggled into Andrew's side. He woke with me, both of us becoming aware at the same time. I burrowed down deep in the blankets, resting my head back against his shoulder. If the world were to stop now, in this very moment, I'd be forever happy, nestled in Andrew's arms for eternity. Of course, the world would not stop for me. Happiness was never complete without sorrow, and although I'd had enough sorrow and pain to last a lifetime, with all the changes and uncertainty, I doubted Fate was through with me.

The room had a chill to it. The fire Andrew had tended before we went to bed had burned down to a few coals, and winter was steadily invading our cottage sanctuary. Andrew gave me a quick kiss on the cheek then got up to uncover the embers and add fresh wood to both our bedroom and the kitchen fireplaces. *Really need to get central heat in this place before much longer. I'm telling you, we're going to wake up to frozen pipes some morning.* Andrew's thought was filled with visions of ruptured waterlines and broken tile in the shower. It gave me chills just thinking about the possible damage. After Andrew finished stoking our fireplaces, he rejoined me in bed and pulled me onto his chest. It would soon be toasty in the cottage, but until then we'd just have to keep each other warm.

He brushed his cold feet against my warm legs. "Damn it! Andrew!" I yelped and slapped at his chest. He merely gave a mischievous laugh in reply, pulling me closer. He groped my ass, shifting my thighs around his, our cocks rubbing enticingly against each other.

"Ah, Andrew," I moaned and humped against him, seeking friction between us.

"Now this is more like the good morning I had planned." Andrew kneaded my cheeks, his fingers following the crack to lightly brush against my hole. I leaned down and our lips locked. He caressed my lower lip with his tongue, and I opened for him, welcoming him, seeking the taste of him—I couldn't get enough. I ran my fingers through his hair. "Ride me," Andrew growled as we came up for air.

How could I deny a request like that? It was impossible when he gave me everything I wanted. I sat back on his thighs and ran my hands over his chest. His skin felt so very good. He drew me forward and rubbed his hands along my back. I loved the feeling of his calloused fingers.

"I want to eat this ass." Andrew leaned up and nipped at my lips. Visions of Andrew's tongue laving my hole had me turning myself around, shoving impatiently at the blankets. I straddled his shoulders, gaining the most perfect view of Andrew's deep-red, engorged cock. I groaned as he slid his hands up my thighs and gripped my butt, brushing his thumbs across my hole.

My focus began to waver slightly as he rubbed his thumbs against my guardian muscle, but the beautiful erection in front of me was calling my name. Andrew's dick was beautiful—thick and long, the head darkening to a purplish red. Precum leaked from the slit, and I ached to taste him. I braced myself on one arm and took Andrew firmly with the other hand.

"You don't have to—" Andrew gasped as I licked the slit. He tasted salty and a bit bitter, but I liked it. I swirled my tongue around the flared hood, slowly, gently. This was so different from every other blowjob I'd ever been forced to give. I wanted to pleasure Andrew. He wasn't jamming himself down my throat; I controlled this and it was wonderful.

Through our mental connection, I could feel the waves of pleasure flowing through Andrew, sharing in turn the things the man was doing to me. Sex with Andrew was all about wanting to give pleasure and sharing myself. Sure, there was lust—how could there not be? But when he groaned my name, I felt like a god.

"Lance, you're... ah!" Andrew panted as I swallowed down as much of the man as I could take, my fist steadying him but also pumping what I couldn't get down my throat. I was so busy working Andrew's cock that I almost missed the snick of the bottle as he dribbled cool liquid over my quivering anus. I tried to synch my movements to his. As he slowly sank his finger into my channel, I swallowed more of his length, bobbing back up as he withdrew. It gave me something to concentrate on so I didn't blow my load too soon.

I worked his shaft, up and down, making sure to give the head extra attention as I ran my tongue under the flared glans before sinking down along the length. Gently, I raked my teeth along the edge of the skin, careful not to apply too much pressure, just enough to make Andrew groan. He slid a second finger alongside the first into my ass. Andrew's hips trembled. He was trying to restrain himself from thrusting and wildly fucking my mouth. I could practically hear him reciting some sort of mathematical equations in his mind in an effort to maintain control. When a third finger entered my ass, I groaned as I deep-throated his cock. The complete body shiver I felt under me let me know just how close to the edge my lover teetered. I grasped his balls and squeezed gently, sucking him hard. He took hold of my waist and lifted me off him with a pop. He spun me around so I once again faced him.

"Inside… I want to come inside, pounding into you, watching you ride me." I heard the snick of the bottle again as I leaned forward, crouching over his hips. I felt the brush of the head of his cock as he teased me, rubbing it against my sensitive hole.

"Don't tease, Andrew. I want it, give it to me," I begged. Bracing myself on his stomach as he held steady, I eased back, impaling myself on him. "Andrew," I gasped as he pressed in and froze. The burn was intense, but good. I wanted the ache. I walked my hands from Andrew's chest to his abs, straightening my body as he sank deeper, brushing over my prostate. "Gahhh… Andrew!" It felt so good.

"You're so hot and tight." Andrew ground his hips up into me, trying to get deeper. I leaned forward and got my feet under me. Then, bracing myself on his chest with his hands on my hips to help me balance, I eased up off him then slammed back down hard. He felt huge, filling me so completely I was sure he could feel my heart beating.

We found our rhythm, me rocking upward while he drew down, flesh slapping as our bodies came together. Our feelings were one; the pleasure he took from me as real as the bliss I found in him. My body tingled with every stroke as he slid against my prostate, pulling me down to meet his every thrust.

"Come for me," Andrew screamed, pounding up into my ass.

"Andrew!" I panted, my orgasm blindsiding me. There was none of the slow burn and tightening of my balls against my body. It was as if I'd just been waiting for him to command it. I collapsed backward against his raised thighs as he shot his load up into me. My cum spattered over his abdomen and chest as he pumped into me. I clenched my ass, hearing his groan I milked him for every hot, slick drop before falling forward onto his chest and into his arms.

I lay, totally sated, in my mate's arms. He played with my hair with his fingers. We stayed motionless, his cock tucked in my ass. I didn't want to move lest he slide from me. I wanted to keep him inside, and yet Andrew was always with me. He lived in my heart and his mind joined with mine. We were never truly separated.

I love you, my mate, Andrew's thoughts whispered to mine.

"I love you too," I told him. *Don't ever leave me. I'd never survive alone.*

"I'm not going anywhere, leannan." Andrew held me tight, but gently eased himself from my body and rolled me to the side. "But as much as I love being inside you, we do have a guest coming today." Andrew got up out of bed and went into the bathroom. I heard the sink running and I closed my eyes. I refused to let the euphoria go. I didn't want the world to intrude on our time.

Andrew returned with a warm washcloth, and I let him clean me up. "I love how you smell."

"I stink of sweat and sex," I mumbled, a sappy grin on my face.

"You smell of sweat, sex, and me. I like it." I couldn't help but chuckle at my besotted lover. "Come on, time to get a move on." Andrew went back into the bathroom and started the shower.

Sandy would be joining us at the farm today. We'd need to discuss her thoughts on the royals and on where she thought this train wreck of a rebellion should go. I also wanted her opinion on how to handle the upcoming confrontation with Stephon. I liked Sandy. Her straightforward attitude and outlook impressed me and made me feel comfortable. It was as if she sensed what was needed in a situation, a skill I desperately wanted to learn. I promised myself I'd ask her to stay and advise me if things ever got to the point where I had to seek out counsel. I didn't like to think that far ahead, especially when I didn't know if I'd survive the day. Granted, a day at the ranch in the company of Sandy and my family wasn't likely to end in bloodshed. I was turning maudlin.

The muted morning light permeating the window over the bed meant the day was heavily overcast with thick gray clouds, a clear threat of rain. I didn't want to move. We were running out of time and each moment we found to love one another began to feel like stolen seconds. Part of me constantly lived in fear that someone would come in the door and rip Andrew from my arms. Of course if they did, they'd be facing a really pissed-off polar bear—or another one of the predators in my arsenal, all possessed of fangs and claws, more than enough to defend what belonged to me. The thought amused Andrew as he washed his hair in the shower.

No one has the power to separate us, leannan. I'm not going anywhere.

We belonged together and no amount of pulling or distance between us would ever take us away from each other.

I got out of bed, deciding I didn't want to have Sandy coming up to the cottage looking for us. Knowing her, she'd walk right into the bedroom and sit on the edge of the bed and we'd have our conversation right here, regardless of what the two of us were occupied with at the time. The picture of Andrew balls-deep in my ass, Sandy sitting at the edge of the bed chatting, amused me and horrified Andrew. His reverence and awe for Sandy, because of her age and the position she held in the family, couldn't stand up to the grandmotherly feelings I seemed to have for her. To me she was what everyone's grandmother should be like—warm, mischievously impish, looking out for her family's best interests and giving them all hell at the same time. I could also envision her as very vicious if someone ever threatened her loved ones. Andrew saw her more in accordance with that image, though he saw her as a grandmotherly figure too, just not quite as warm and fuzzy as I did.

With the temperatures dropping, I decided to wear something I could travel in. Stephon could be sending for us... soon. I could feel Andrew's certainty, even without asking. He felt it'd be sooner than later. After choosing a pair of heavy khakis, a white button-down shirt, and a thick red sweater, I dressed and headed for the bathroom to tame my unruly hair and brush my teeth. I wet my hair down and pulled the comb through the length, catching and pulling on the knots. *I need to get my hair cut. It's becoming a pain.* The almost instantaneous denial of the thought from Andrew made me bite the inside of my lip to keep the smirk from my face.

"You will not. I love your hair." Andrew came up behind me and took the comb from my hand. With a few careful strokes, he gathered my hair and drew it back against the nape of my neck. He tied it away from my face with a strip of leather, freeing me of the frustrating tendrils. "Better?"

"Yes. Thank you." We were both getting edgy, not knowing from one minute to the next how much time we had before we'd be swept away to defend Andrew's right to be free. I turned and noticed he wore khakis as well, along with a cream-colored sweater. The contrast between the cream of the sweater and his golden skin and black hair took my breath away. He leaned in and kissed me. He knew how much I enjoyed looking at him.

Having banked the fires in the grates, we left our cottage sanctuary, not knowing if or when we'd be able to return.

Renovations for the future had taken a backseat to the insanity in our lives, but we'd remember to tell his dad and brothers about getting a furnace installed there soon. As we went out the door, I looked longingly back at my sanctuary, missing it already.

Charlie approached as we exited the cottage. She looked better today than she had yesterday. I hadn't really gotten a good look at her new outfit in the dark, but today she wore heavy black leathers over a black turtleneck sweater. A black baseball cap was pulled down tight with a ponytail pulled through the gap in the back. A pair of dark glasses finished off the look. From the four corners of the meadow, four more vampires approached at a quick trot. At first I thought we were under attack, but then I realized these must be some of the guards Tim had called for her. They took up ranks behind her. She seemed much calmer now that her reinforcements had arrived. I smiled at her and she actually smiled back…. Okay, Charlie obviously felt *very* relaxed.

"Off to the farm for your meeting with Sandy?" Charlie asked.

"Yes," Andrew answered. I watched as he closely inspected the black-clad vampires standing behind her.

"These are some of the warriors Tim called for me yesterday. There are more out in the woods, a total of ten. There'll be no more surprise attacks," she said with confidence. Through our mental link, I could feel Andrew's relief. "We'll move around the ranch. Some are already there, scouting ahead."

"Will you come in to the meeting?" I tentatively asked. "I'd like to hear your point of view. I really appreciate anything you can add."

"Just try and stop me. I'm not letting either of you out of my sight." Charlie's fanged grin sent a chill of foreboding down my spine.

The three of us got into the truck and headed to the ranch. I wasn't sure when it happened, but when I looked around, the rest of the guard had disappeared into the trees. The thought that I missed them leaving made me feel uneasy. I needed to become more observant. Too many things were getting past me.

When we arrived, Sandy sat on the porch swing, gently rocking, with Angela seated on her lap. Andrew's cousin and best friend, Sam, was also there, along with nine other men scattered about, chatting in small groups.

"Good. About time you arrived. I was just about to come and get you myself," Sandy scolded, setting Angela on her feet.

"They're here!" Angela opened the screen door and hollered at the top of her lungs as she ran inside.

"Did you eat before you came?" Sandy took my arm as Andrew opened the door and held it for us.

"No, we haven't eaten." I winked at Andrew. He blushed slightly. I could hear him thinking about what we'd been doing instead of eating.

"Well, Laura's been cooking like crazy since we all started arriving. Let's go get the two of you fed." She patted my hand and Andrew's cheek. Her grandmotherly touch sent warm feelings of love and family coursing through me in ways I'd never experienced before. She led the way and I could only nod as I tried to choke back the tears that threatened to fall. These people surrounded me, cared about me, and I would make sure nothing ever hurt them. They were my family.

Sandy, Andrew, and I walked into the yellow kitchen. It was practically filled to capacity. The twins made room at the table for Andrew and me while Max gave up his seat to Sandy so she could sit across from us.

Laura smiled and hummed as she cooked, making breakfast for everyone. She set down plates filled with scrambled eggs, bacon, hash browns, and toast in front of us, followed by a cup of tea for me and coffee for Andrew.

"Thank you so much. This smells wonderful."

"Thanks, Mom." Andrew grinned up at Laura.

"You know me… people start arriving, I cook." She tousled our hair like we were children and then moved off to fill the coffee cups of a couple other men sitting at the table, men I had yet to meet.

The conversation was light and friendly, everyone enjoying the camaraderie before getting down to the business that drew us together. The twins taunted Andrew and Sam while Sandy gave Max a hard time about trying to find mates for his younger sons. Andrew mentioned needing a furnace for the cottage to his dad. In his wisdom, Max had already ordered one. Many of the men moved outside in an attempt to make room in the overcrowded kitchen. It was wonderful, and to my surprise, I didn't feel out of place in the least. The claustrophobia and fear of people that normally plagued me wasn't present here.

Charlie stood at the back, trying to be unobtrusive while keeping Andrew and me in sight. I could tell by the way she shuffled her feet and crossed her arms that she wasn't exactly comfortable with the number of strange shifters in the room. The family kept drawing her into conversations, making sure she was included and not ostracized as the only vampire in the room. But their attention made her fidget more, increasing her anxiety instead of easing the stress of the moment. They'd adopted her into the fold. She had been there to defend us and that made her part of the family—whether she wanted to be or not. Like me, she was going to have to get used to the new state of things, and it made me smile to know I wasn't the only one trying to deal with the change.

"Now, if everyone will excuse me, I'm going to take this munchkin upstairs. We have lessons to go over." Laura nodded to her husband as she scooped Angela off Jack's lap, who was seated in the corner, and carried her from the room.

"I never get to hear the good stuff," Angela complained as the two headed down the hall to a chorus of chuckles from those who remained. Many more followed them out, leaving Sandy, Sam, Max, Jack and Joe, Charlie, Andrew and myself, along with a man I was unfamiliar with.

"Okay, kids, what's on your mind?" Sandy's scrutiny changed in an instant from grandmotherly to that of a wary leader. Andrew slid closer to me and squeezed my thigh under the table.

"We have some very big obstacles coming up on us fast, Sandy." I closed my eyes briefly as the magnitude of everything sitting on my shoulders assailed me. "I'm really not sure what I should be doing. I know what my instincts tell me to do, but I'm not sure what's best. My main concern is for my mate, but I can't just free Andrew and disappear." I looked at my family—Max, Jack, Joe, and Sam—then back to meet Sandy's eyes. "I have a family. For the first time I have something to fight for."

"We won't let you do it alone. That's part of what being a family is all about, son. Even if we can't stand beside you every step of the way, know that you are never alone," Max reassured me as he reached across the table and squeezed my hand. I nodded, bolstered by his belief in me.

"I don't like the condition our people are in. I think even if we were to run, eventually we'd have to come back." I nodded to myself. "I couldn't leave my family bound to a vampire, unable to make their own decisions." I met Andrew's eyes and felt his encouragement and pride. It hadn't been that long ago I'd been afraid to be with Max, much less in a room full of people like this, speaking my mind. "Everyone should have the opportunity to make their own decisions. The time for benefactors is past—if the need ever existed in the first place. Dr. Tim assures me our population is no longer in danger of extinction, and self-determination should not be a problem. I trust his assessment. He says the animal in each of us naturally seeks a stronger mate, and if left to our own devices, we'd eventually rebuild our bloodlines to pureblood status naturally. Each of us seeks a mate to complement our own strengths and weaknesses." I let that thought sink in.

"Tim believes some families are stronger than others. Among the benefactors there are some who've worked to build, or at least maintain, the strengths of the families in their care, while others have purposefully destroyed bloodlines. Stephon is believed to be one who's tried to better the shifter families in his charge. I don't know how many families there are, what condition they're in, or what needs they have, but I believe the matriarch of each family would know. The best way to rebuild would be to have the matriarchs form a council to make decisions for our people as a whole, for them to jointly rule." I stared into Sandy's eyes. I could practically see the gears turning in her mind at all the possibilities I'd shown her.

"I… I don't…," Sandy stuttered, at a bit of a loss for words.

"I'm no leader, Sandy. I never even finished high school." I sighed self-consciously. "A year ago I didn't even know shifters and vampires existed. I don't know how to lead a people. I'm still learning who I am." I threw my hands up in the air. "I certainly can't walk into Stephon's demanding Andrew's freedom and the Right to Rule without at least having something to offer in return. Well, at least some kind of a plan…." My wolf wanted to pace, but there were so many people in the kitchen there wasn't room. "I don't know how quickly things will move once people discover who and what I am. For all I know, Stephon's the least of my concerns. Even if I'm successful with him, I'll have the royal family to deal with, and my suspicion is they'll be more of a headache than an actual ally. Finally, there'll be the Vampire

Council. I hardly expect the leaders who created the beneficiary program will want it questioned, much less allow it to be abolished." I held out a pleading hand to her. "Please, Sandy, I need your wisdom. I'm at a loss here. Are these the right decisions for our people? Maybe I'm wrong and freedom *isn't* what you really want. Should I just free Andrew and disappear?" I shook my head, lost in confusion and frustration.

Sandy took my hand and squeezed tightly. "Oh, to be so young and have such responsibility piled upon you. You have a good heart to be willing to take on the burden of seeking freedom for us all. Our people are naturally free spirits and caretakers. We'll never truly be ourselves until we're free." Sandy's smile reassured me as only Andrew's thoughts and touch had ever done.

"Do I think you're making the right decision in seeking to free Andrew? Yes, undoubtedly. With seeking freedom for us all? Also yes. Of course there will be some who won't thank you." A look of utter disgust crossed Sandy's face. "Some have forgotten who we are. Freedom takes work. Just because we *can* make our own decisions doesn't mean it will be easy to do so. They've become complacent and sedentary, accepting the scraps handed to them while they let others make all their decisions for them. They've become selfish, wallowing in ignorance, refusing to see beyond their blinders. Life will become suddenly much more difficult for them when they have to fend for themselves."

"We're all children of Mother Nature. Her way has ever been survival of the fittest." Max's determination shone through in the stern set of his jaw.

"We'll grow or die. It's not a pleasant thought, and it won't happen overnight." Sandy paused, choosing her words carefully. "I like the idea of a Matriarchal Council because ultimately the mothers of our people are the ones who head our families. They know best what our families are capable of. But many matriarchs may not want to leave their families to be on such a council—especially under such uncertain conditions." Sandy paused, gazing off, deep in thought. "I'd amend the council to the matriarch or their chosen family representative, with maybe the eldest matriarch or her representative as leader of the council."

"That's a good idea. Offering an alternative in case the matriarch can't get away, but still giving the family representation." Max fiddled with his coffee cup, considering the idea. "Each family has land they protect and are tied to. Some acquired land after the war, while others owned the land before the war and the treaty. You'll need to make sure we don't lose the land we occupy. No good for the family to be free if we lose our land to the vampire benefactors. They could basically hold the land hostage to force our obedience. We must have a territory to be whole."

I understood the pull of territory. My sanctuary and the meadow around it were my territory; although since I'd come to love Andrew's family, their ranch and all of the land around it also felt like my territory, though realistically I understood it belonged to Max and I'd never challenge his authority for it.

"Would you be willing to come with me when I go to the royals?" I asked Sandy. "I really want someone with me who I can trust to advise me. I won't go without Andrew, but neither of us knows the politics of how these things work. Tim and Charlie will also be there. They've got some experience with politics, but they are still outsiders and don't know our ways. I don't want to fumble around blindly and make a fool of myself when I don't know how much time I'll have to get their cooperation. I already have enemies, but no idea who they are. I'd like to have as many friendly eyes as I can get to watch out for me."

Sandy squeezed my hand gently. "I'd be honored to go with you and assist in dealing with the royals. You *are* part of my family, after all. I should be there. While you're away dealing with Stephon, I'll try and ferret out which families will be supporters and which we'll have to keep an eye on." Sandy turned to Charlie. "I know you serve as vassal to Lance and Andrew, and that you head their guard. I've brought ten men to add to his guard from our family. Sam, of course, is amongst them and he's one of the best. Other than Sam's eagle, they're all wolves and very strong."

"Thank you. That will increase our number to twenty. We should be able to watch both the cottage and the ranch twenty-four hours a day now." Charlie nodded. You could practically see her working out guard rotations in her mind and spinning scenarios as to our best defense.

Sandy turned back to me. "Now, for a bit of a shifter lesson. Out of the fifteen major families, I'd say probably five families are strong like ours. These five families are split among four benefactors. One of them, as you know, is Stephon. Another is Quinn—he is the other benefactor many members of our family belong to. The names of the other two born vampires involved are not known to me. Among the other ten families, some are stagnant, but most are slowly disintegrating. The royal family is among the most decimated of the bloodlines. *You* are the only viable shifter in that family line. They can no longer hear when the beast speaks and most can't hold an animal shape longer than an hour or two. Most will die in a human lifespan because their blood's so diluted they're more human than shifter." Sandy closed her eyes and shook her head at the thought.

"Do you think those families will die out? Are they beyond help?" Max asked, sounding shocked that only a third of their community might survive.

"If we're selective, we may be able to salvage some of the bloodlines, but only if we can find some among them who are strong enough. Of the five strong families, the branches are many, and there are dozens of strong healthy children. We'll be able to choose some and send them to universities and get them educations so they can bring back the knowledge to strengthen us. And I suspect there'll be drones like Tim and Charlie who will be willing to help. There'll definitely be obstacles." Sandy smiled and patted my hand sympathetically. "But the outcome, if you succeed, will be worth the effort."

The man I'd never met spoke up, with a touch of awe in his voice. "Freedom is worth the price. To be able to choose my own mate… to send my children to college… to just be able to live and not have to be concerned whether a choice I make will anger my benefactor…. I can't even tell you what that's worth to me."

"My grandson, Jericho Stone," Sandy said, introducing the man, who nodded to me. "To be honest, Lance, the most you can offer us is the opportunity. Once you set things in place, it'll be up to us to do the work and make the decisions. Yes, the Vampire Council will make demands. They might want you to head the Matriarch Council for some kind of trial time frame, but I do believe if each family gets equal representation, it will be a sound government model for us. Once the Matriarch Council takes over the job of leading our people into the future, you should be able to take Andrew and have a worry-free honeymoon, all to yourselves."

"I hope so. All of this is so overwhelming for me. I'd really like to just be able to spend some time alone with my mate."

"I know, and you will. Mother Nature's a tough mistress, so I fully expect the two of you to make many babies. We can't have the two strongest among us not passing on their genes to the rest of our people. Surrogates are not unheard of among our people, and since the breeding programs, families like Laura and Max are rare. Many families exist where not all the children have the same father or mother. I want to watch your children grow and prosper and add to the strength of our people." Sandy chuckled, and I practically blanched at the thought. Children of our own! I couldn't think past today, much less to a future where Andrew and I had babies running around.

"I don't know, Sandy. Children? That's a bit far off in the future, don't you think? But, thank you. It means a great deal to me knowing you're willing to commit so much to this." My uneasy thoughts about children had shaken me to the core, even though the idea of having a child with Andrew appealed to a part of me I hadn't even realized I possessed. I just couldn't bring a child into this turmoil and insanity better known as my life. Maybe someday....

It's okay, leannan. I feel the same way. A child with you—either yours, mine, or both—would be a blessing. I know Angela is too young right now, but maybe by the time we are ready, she might be willing to donate an egg, so a surrogate could carry a child of your line and mine. But not until we make this world safe. Andrew's sentiments mirrored my own. Not because we shared our thoughts, but because we both wanted our child to be safe and free.

"I feel so much better knowing you're with me, that you'll guide me through the parts I don't understand," I told Sandy. Her agreement to help had lifted a weight off my shoulders. Sandy would be invaluable in making the difficult decisions.

"Andrew, Lance, if you don't mind, I'm going to have Sam introduce me to the other men we'll be adding to your security detail," Charlie remarked, seemingly happy about the idea of a larger force.

"Sure, Charlie, I'll go with you." Andrew rose beside me and kissed me on the head. I watched as my family and Sandy's grandson headed out the kitchen door, leaving Sandy and me alone.

"Are you happy, young one?" Sandy came around the table and sat beside me.

"Extremely. I worry about him, though. I'm positive when he fell in love with that stray who showed up outside his home, he never dreamed I'd be this much trouble." I smiled self-consciously. "I've added so much stress to his life, yet he loves me totally and unconditionally."

"That's wonderful. You are going to need each other if we are to succeed." Sandy rubbed my hand.

"I've grown in so many ways, I hardly recognize myself sometimes. But when I struggle, he's there to remind me of who I am." It was easy to wax poetic about Andrew. He was my rock.

"How have you grown? Max said you chose a fourth form, and rather on the fly, if I understand the circumstances of your encounter with David and the drones."

"Andrew has three forms, and I shifted into a forth when we were attacked last night. After the first time we were attacked and the twins were with us, when Jack had been hurt, we discovered my saliva had healing properties. It's also acidic to drones, although that seems to be a characteristic I can turn on and off, as I was able to help Charlie heal after the attack last night."

"These things you say you can do have been noted in the histories as abilities of our ancestors—strengths we've never shared about ourselves with the vampires. It's right that they should be surfacing in you. More may appear as time passes; the histories speak of many gifts. I don't know if our ancestors had all of them or if each person had special gifts." Sandy grinned. "It will be interesting to see what manifests. If you have questions, always feel you can come to me."

"Andrew has grown in his own abilities. Tim believes Andrew's as strong as I am now. He said before we mated that once we did, we'd be stronger together."

"Oh my, he's showing signs of pureblood?"

I nodded. "When we became mated and merged our minds, it felt like we became two parts of one whole being. Our power and abilities are shared, just as our minds are. We shift in the same way, and I feel like we could be anything we wish." I closed my eyes and took a deep breath. "There's so much I'm learning as I go. Between the things Andrew overlooks and the new stuff, the powers nobody seemed to know about—sometimes I feel so lost. And yet, knowing what I know now about what a pureblood shifter means to our people... I wonder if I'd have survived growing up within our society any better than I did among humans. At least there I lived to tell about it. Between the vampires who feel threatened by my existence and those with a grudge against my family, I'm not sure I'd have survived my childhood."

"Well, you have a matriarch now, so if you have any questions, I'll be close by. You can ask me anything at all. Even if I don't know the answers, I'll try to help any way I can." Sandy patted my hand sharply. "In fact, I know the Fenrir family had extensive holdings and a large home territory at one time. I'll see if I can find out what happened to them. I'm sure it's all gone now, probably divided up by the vampires as spoils after the war. There should also be Lord Nathaniel's holdings. You'll be the only heir to his properties, and inherit them as you did his vassals. Knowing Tim, I'm sure he's looking into who's currently holding his lord's estate for you." Sandy draped an arm around my waist. "You'll have many options once things calm down. Then you and Andrew can have the peaceful life you both crave. One step at a time, child. Don't let it overwhelm you." Sandy stood, took my hand, and drew me to my feet, then placed her arm in mine. We walked through the house and out onto the porch.

The controlled chaos outdoors surprised me. Charlie had the men going through their paces, judging their individual strengths and weaknesses. Tim had arrived at some point and sat on the steps beside Andrew. A couple of vampire warriors had been called in to help with the testing. Of course the twins were right in the thick of things, absorbing everything they could.

"Come on, we're old enough. We can do everything they can!" Jack insisted, arguing with Max and Charlie.

"So what if we're smaller? We're faster too. *And* we've already fought vampires. Let us help," Joe begged.

"It's up to you, Charlie. You think they can keep up with your warriors?" Max asked.

"Fine, get out there with the rest of them, you cubs." Charlie shook her head. She waved over one of the vampires who'd been standing at the back. "Keep an eye on them. They're just cubs, and I don't want them hurt." The warrior nodded, and after putting an arm on each of the cubs, led them back to his spot at the back of the pack.

"Are you sure about this?" Andrew watched as his little brothers began to work out with the vampire Charlie had assigned to them.

"They're young and inexperienced, but not incapable. It'll be good for them to develop some skills we can use around here. Namely, guard duty on the road." Charlie's eyes twinkled with amusement. I was sure the twins wouldn't relish standing at the edge of the driveway watching for intruders.

"Oh, Charlie, they won't thank you for that." Max roared with laughter, and we all joined in, knowing the twins had dreams of glory, not playing sentry. Still, the training would be good for them. They needed discipline and a firm hand to curb their teenage rebellion. It'd also keep them busy and out of trouble during the winter months ahead.

CHAPTER 9

EVERYTHING stopped as a black Mercedes with tinted windows pulled into the driveway. My guards, both vampire and shifter, took up defensive positions around the yard as Charlie, Sam, Tim, and two others surrounded Andrew and me. Thunder rumbled ominously from the darkening storm clouds that had been building most of the day. We watched as two vampires in black suits got out of the car. It was all very Mafia-esque and if my life weren't hanging in the balance, I might have cracked up, laughing at the drama. One opened the back door, and I halfway expected a large, fat man to emerge; instead a slim blonde stepped from the vehicle.

Victoria, Andrew whispered in my mind.

The woman was stunningly beautiful. She'd pulled her long, shiny blonde hair back from her pale oval face. She wore a black power suit jacket with a tight, matching miniskirt that had less length than a pair of daisy dukes, a white blouse that hung daringly open to her pierced navel, and a pair of stiletto heels. Dark sunglasses hid her eyes, even though the evening light escaping the storm clouds was already weak. In this setting—surrounded by heavy-duty ranch equipment, bawling cows and the distinct scent of manure—she looked utterly ridiculous as she walked across the gravel driveway, getting her shoes dusty.

"That's Victoria, Stephon's personal assistant. I'm guessing she's been sent to get us," Andrew softly informed Tim and Charlie.

Victoria strutted her way across the yard as if life was her personal catwalk, heading for the steps, a guard at either side of her. At the foot of the porch steps, she looked up over the top of her sunglasses at Andrew and me. We stood between Charlie and Tim, surrounded by various vampires and shape-shifters, some in animal form.

"Andrew, please be a dear and get your things together. I'm assuming he's the one you call mate?" She looked at me disdainfully, fluttering a hand in my direction as if I were an insignificant thing created to bother her. A soft growl started in the back of my throat, but I could hear Charlie growling a far louder warning. Charlie wasn't impressed with Victoria. The woman's attitude and dress screamed "blonde bimbo," and if I'd seen her on the street, I'd have added "expensive whore."

"Stephon wants to see you. You know how I hate it when he sends me on errands," she mumbled, rolling her eyes as she inspected her manicure.

"I'd be happy to break one of those nails for her," I mumbled, soft enough only Charlie and Andrew could hear me.

Charlie stopped growling and started giggling uncontrollably. We all turned to look at her while she struggled to regain her composure before she lost all her dangerous bad-girl points.

"We'll be right with you, Victoria. Why don't you relax in your car? You'll be more comfortable there while we say our good-byes to our family." Andrew eyed Charlie, an eyebrow raised in amusement.

"Fine, just don't keep me waiting. I want to leave." She made her way back to the car and disappeared into the tinted interior. How I prayed one of those stilettos would get stuck in a hole or break off, but no such luck.

Her guards retreated to the car with her, but stood outside it to wait for us. We'd known Stephon would send someone. I just… I wasn't ready.

Tim got the four-wheel-drive Dodge Ram from the barn and pulled it into the drive for us. We'd planned on Tim and Charlie, along with four others, following us, acting as my personal guard. We bid good-bye to our family. Charlie seemed to have taken Sam on as her second-in-command. She gave him instructions for the wolves and the remaining vampire guards. We weren't sure how long we were going to be gone, but it wasn't like we didn't have cell phones to contact anyone we needed.

"Lance, use your charm with Stephon," Sandy said. "If what Tim said is true, he should be susceptible. Flattery will get you everywhere where Stephon's concerned. You just need to treat him more like one of the girls. Remember, you need an ally, not an enemy. I'd come with you if I could, but I don't dare. We aren't allowed to visit the home of a born vampire without an express invitation." Sandy smiled at me and patted my hands then threw her arms around me and gave me a big hug. She pulled me down to her level and kissed the top of my head, then said good-bye to Andrew in the same way.

Andrew clapped Sam on the back in a manly hug.

"You'll be fine. Charlie will look out for you," Laura whispered, trying to reassure both me and herself.

"We'll be fine," I repeated, although the butterflies in my stomach were becoming more agitated the longer this good-bye seemed to take.

Max took over as soon as Laura released me. He didn't say a word, just held me tight while Andrew said good-bye to his mom. Jack and Joe hugged me from both sides, my favorite twin sandwich. "I'll miss you guys. Take care of my cottage."

"We will. We wanted to come too, but Dad said no," Jack grumbled in my ear.

"He needs you here while Andrew's away. Besides, you have training to do with the vampires."

"Okay," they chorused, each twin resting a chin on one of my shoulders.

We were passed around until everyone had said their good-byes. Once finished, we hurried to the truck. I climbed into the passenger's seat while Andrew settled in on the driver's side. One of Victoria's guards approached Andrew's door.

"You are to go straight to the house. We'll make sure you're on your way up the trail. After that, others will be watching." The vampire scowled menacingly, his voice deep and gruff. Andrew just rolled his eyes.

"Maurice, please, enough with the bad-guy stuff. I told you ages ago—you don't do it well. Maybe you should try an Italian accent, give it a Mafia feel. Just a thought." Andrew tried not to laugh as disappointment flared on the vampire's face.

"Aw, I really thought I had it that time," he said in a much more nasally and higher-pitched voice, and then he pouted as he headed back to the car, stomping his feet in a minitantrum.

I looked at Andrew, my eyebrows raised in amusement.

"Don't ask." He laughed. "You really don't want to know."

The Mercedes took off down the road, and we followed. A black Suburban shadowed us. I assumed it was Tim, Charlie, and our four guards.

I'd been going over Andrew's memories and impressions of Stephon. I could tell my lover thought of Stephon as eccentric. The vampire dressed colorfully, and his interests were varied—interior decorating, acting, gardening, books, fashion, endless formal parties—and those were just the beginning. Andrew also thought of him as family—of sorts. Not family like the type you could rely on to bring you soup if you got sick, but more the crazy uncle you tolerated and whose faults you put up with good-naturedly because it was expected. I had one thought: high maintenance.

"How far is it to Stephon's?" I asked Andrew.

"We'll be at the trailhead in a couple of hours, then the climb takes about an hour to run. We could get there much faster if we flew, but Tim and Charlie believe we really need to impress upon Stephon that they're part of our lives." Andrew sighed. My man just wanted this to be over. "A united front, as Tim called it. They want Stephon to know they take their jobs as vassals seriously." I could tell he doubted Stephon would free him, regardless of the stance we took or the forms we could take. Ultimately we were shifters and had to have a benefactor—end of story.

"Don't lose hope, love. We haven't even asked him yet. I told you I'd try very hard not to kill him. Everyone seems to think he isn't the ogre I see him as. I'm hoping you're all right."

"Stephon's exceedingly hard to explain to someone. He's… complicated." Andrew shook his head. I could see him picture Stephon in his mind. The man appeared to be shorter than Andrew, with thick, curly blond hair dovetailed in the front and large curls around his ears. The oddest thing was his eyes.

"Does he really have violet eyes?" I asked, unable to remember ever seeing anyone with eyes that color.

"Yes. The born vampires I've met over the years all have kind of ethereal-colored eyes that kind of glow in the dark like a cat. Only drones have black eyes." It seemed born vampires might be very different from the drones I'd met so far.

I had to smile at the image of the house in the mountains, the one we were heading to, as I viewed it among Andrew's memories. It was a white three-story colonial with an enclosed wraparound porch, complete with a white picket fence and arched, rose-covered trellised walkways, along with a gazebo in the backyard. It looked like a feature home on the cover of *Better Homes and Gardens*. Stephon had obviously missed the memo saying villains and evil slave owners needed to reside in dungeons, caves or at the very least in Grecian-pillared plantation mansions. Seriously, the house could have been more aligned with a horror story... not Martha Stewart. In fact, I couldn't imagine any self-respecting vampire living in such a suburban-looking home, though I'd yet to see where Tim or Charlie lived, so I had nothing to compare it to.

The sky rumbled and rain began to fall. The sound of the windshield wipers flicking back and forth beat out the passing of time. The miles seemed to crawl by under the tires of the truck. I took off my seat belt—it kept me too far from Andrew—and scooted across to curl up next to him on the bench seat. Andrew draped his arm across my shoulders and snuggled me up against his body, pillowing my head on his thigh.

"Sleep. It'll be a while before we get there." Andrew stroked my hair, settling my nerves. The constant hum of the tires with the wipers lulled me into a light sleep.

I WOKE when the truck slowed and turned. The crunch of gravel under the tires alerted me that we were no longer on the highway. The gray day remained, but rain no longer fell. I still felt just as gloomy. I saw the Mercedes had pulled off to the side of the gravel road. We had passed it by. The Suburban followed us farther up the dirt road to the dead end.

"The trail's unmarked. He doesn't like uninvited visitors." Andrew pulled to a stop under some overhanging tree branches and we got out. I stretched and yawned. Tim and Charlie, along with the four vampire guards, joined us. They somehow managed to look just as fresh as they had when they'd first arrived at the farm. I had no doubt they'd look just as fresh when we arrived at the top of the mountain. Of course, running came second nature to me, and after riding in the truck all those miles, I needed to stretch my legs. Flying would've been better, but running would do.

Andrew nodded at our guard and then took my hand as we headed into the forest. I could feel how much Andrew enjoyed running here. It felt kind of like a homecoming for him. He also looked forward to seeing Stephon, despite the arguments that were bound to take place. He really did think of Stephon as family and wanted him to like me.

You think we should've made the others wait for us at home. I said, realizing it was a bit too late to convince them to go back now.

It's excessive and unnecessary, but then again, Stephon thrives on extravagance, so maybe they're right in thinking that the show of guards will impress him. It just seems a bit silly to me. From what Tim said, the council forced him to take on the shifters. He might not be able to free me even if he wants to. Andrew's thoughts were troubled, and I could tell he was hesitant to press for his freedom if it would cost someone else theirs.

You think the vampire council will punish him if he grants your freedom. I was shocked at the fear and pain that thought caused my mate. His feelings for Stephon went deeper than I'd realized.

127

They could demand his life. They could consider it treason against his race for him to free me against their spoken wishes. Stephon would end up forfeiting his life for my freedom, and I'd never ask him to do that. I could see his point. If the council could force Stephon to take on shifters all those years ago, why should it be any different today?

Don't give up without even asking. We have to try. That's all we can do. I wrapped the thoughts in all my love for him as we ran.

He gave my hand a brief squeeze. "I love you too."

Andrew felt grateful I'd freed him from Stephon being in his head, but he didn't believe we could win this particular battle and was afraid to hope for his freedom. He'd rebelled for years as a juvenile shifter for want of the freedom to make his own choices. I'd seen his memories and the punishments he'd suffered by order of the Vampire Council. Stephon's enforcer had been Andrew's Uncle David, who'd taken great pleasure in doling out punishment. Andrew had learned to not want freedom under the bite of his uncle's whip. I could understand his reluctance to even hope.

The thing about hope, though, is sometimes the smallest dreams can blossom into wondrous gifts. I showed him the small piece of hope I'd had for a warm place to keep the snow out and how what was once a broken-down miner's cabin in the woods had become our beautiful sanctuary. All because I had a tiny piece of hope. Andrew smiled and laughed, pulling me to a stop to kiss me.

"Thank you for reminding me." Then we took off together at a quicker pace. He'd become excited; if he couldn't hope, he'd allow me to hope for the both of us.

I could see the clearing ahead. Andrew slowed down and looked at me, then at Tim and Charlie. They nodded encouragement and smiled. I had no doubt we were being watched and that private conversation at this point would be impossible—well, for all except Andrew and me. As we cleared the tree line, I saw just what I expected to see.

The house looked as though it had been plucked right out of Martha's Vineyard and transplanted on top of this mountain. A blond man stood along the side of the house. I could tell, even from a distance, that he was impeccably dressed. His clothing, tailored specifically for him, accentuated a strong lean body. He wore white slacks and a sea-foam-green, long-sleeved shirt. The buttons at his neckline were open; a single heavy, ornate gold chain hung at his throat, precisely across his collarbones. He wore a gardening apron decorated with pink flowers and matching sea-foam-green leaves. Gardening tools, a pair of clippers and spade with matching pink handles, hung from loops on the apron. His curly blond hair shone even in the gray, cloudy morning light. His skin was so pale it almost seemed translucent, but the violet eyes, gazing upon us as if he was trying to see through us, caught and held my attention. This could be none other than Stephon.

He was everything I'd expected and more. We ran on until we reached the yard, stopping a few feet from where he stood, having turned back to his roses. Slowly, as if he hadn't watched us approach, he turned from them, and a beautiful smile lit his face when he saw Andrew.

"Well, hi, Poodle," Stephon greeted Andrew with a wave. "I'm so glad you were able to come and visit. You're looking good, much better than when I last saw you. A little shaggy, though, don't you think?" He brushed at his hair. "Maybe I can call Filipe and have him squeeze you in for a wash and clip while you're here." Stephon stepped away from the flowers and put a hand on each of Andrew's shoulders, then kissed his cheek. "You know how I miss you. I wish you wouldn't stay away so long." Andrew rolled his eyes.

"How are you doing, Stephon?" Andrew seemed a little put out, but he sighed tolerantly at the vampire.

I hadn't realized how shaggy Andrew's hair had become, but I liked it longer. He used to spike it, but now he combed it to the side. It probably could do with a trim, but I hoped he wouldn't go back to the spike.

"Poodle?" I asked Andrew, not quite able to hide the smirk or the chuckle forcing its way out.

"Stephon has always liked his jokes." Andrew shook his head and rolled his eyes again.

I looked a little closer at Stephon and saw what I'd been missing. I'd misjudged the vampire, being caught up in my own preconceptions of what a born vampire would or should be. I'd completely missed the obvious. Stephon was out and proud. He was the kind of man there wasn't a closet large enough to come out of… unless it held his wardrobe, and I could admire that. The bigger issue was that this man carried a torch for my Andrew. The wolf in me snarled, wanting to kill any threat to my mate. Jealousy—that green-eyed monster—wanted to rip Stephon apart. The problem was Andrew saw Stephon as family, and my love had no idea Stephon was in love with him.

"Oh no…." The words escaped my mouth before I could stop them. I heard Charlie snicker behind me, and I spun to see her stifling her giggles while Tim looked on in complete confusion. Why did some men miss the facts presented blatantly before their eyes? Now Sandy's last comment about treating him more like one of the girls made perfect sense. I quickly saw Andrew's refusal to choose a mate from Stephon's point of view and realized from the way his face lit up when he saw Andrew that the vampire hoped eventually, maybe in a century or so, Andrew would be his. Stephon was a jilted crush. I felt Andrew's denial in my mind, refusing to believe what I showed him.

Stephon turned. With his hands clasped to his chest, he looked me over critically, then sighed. "So this is the *little bitch* you think is your mate? He's hardly anything special to look at, Andrew."

"So, you must be the *blood sucker* with a hard-on for my mate," I snarled petulantly back at him. "You've got it so bad you've kept Andrew on a choke chain all these years, hardly considerate of you." He started at my sarcasm. I'd have to come up with a new plan. I wasn't sure how to smooth the ruffled feathers of a vampire suffering from an unrequited love for my man.

Part of me pitied him. He'd spent all those years in love with Andrew and—nothing. Andrew would never love him the way Stephon wanted to be loved. How awful, the unending loneliness of waiting for the right person for centuries, only to find a man you think might come to love you, and have him yanked away. Another part of me just wanted to rip the vampire to shreds. Andrew belonged to me and nobody dared to challenge that and live.

"He's stunningly beautiful, Stephon; surely you can see that." Andrew looked at me, critically at first, and then I felt his adoration wash over me and I smiled back at him. With Andrew looking at me, I could see myself as he saw me, and be anything he wanted me to be. It also served to cool the green-eyed monster rearing its ugly head in my soul.

"But, Poodle, look what he's wearing." Stephon actually stamped his foot in annoyance. "I've taught you about tailoring and designer labels. He doesn't even know how to dress himself! And even though you're handsome as always, love, you could use a bit more care in your clothing choices as well." Andrew seemed a bit taken aback; he'd given me the clothes himself.

"Now, *blood sucker…* hmm, BS—you don't mind if I call you BS, do you?" I snarled at Stephon.

"Well—"

"Nobody insults my gifts. Andrew went to quite a bit of trouble to choose some very nice and functional clothing for me. I guess you could say it's part of my dowry." I smiled lovingly at Andrew, but a little mischievously as well. I began to play to the sarcastic youthful side Stephon had been showing. The vampire was hurt and trying to defend himself, so I'd go along with that and maybe we could come to an understanding of sorts. He couldn't have Andrew. He needed to let go of his dream, though I was sure it wouldn't be easy for the centuries-old vampire.

"Well, as long as I get to call you LB, you *little bitch*," Stephon huffed and then paled. "Oh no, Andrew… you did this." He ran his hand up and down, pointing at my outfit. "Leave it to a male to completely miss the importance of style and design. I'm so sorry, LB. I was sure I'd taught him better." Stephon pouted and glared at Andrew before his eyes softened and got a bit misty. He was put out that he couldn't blame my lack of refinement on my own negligence, but he couldn't be angry with Andrew. I had no interest in designer labels, as my wardrobe had always come to me secondhand. I went for function much more than style. Andrew knew that, and his choices were perfect for me, regardless of what Stephon thought.

Sighing like the greatly beset vampire he was, Stephon motioned to me, scowling. "Well, Andrew believes you to be supremely talented. So let's see it." Stephon pulled his gardening clippers from his apron and waved them around in his hand as if he expected me to transform immediately.

"Oh please, Stephon. You expect me to just drop my drawers right here on your front lawn? How gauche." I placed a hand on my hip and rolled my eyes. "Really, there's a time and place for everything. Surely you don't want a naked man on your front lawn with all these spectators?" I acted surprised he'd suggest such a thing.

"I do see your point. What would people think, a naked man on *my* front lawn?" Stephon shook his head in dismay, but eyed me speculatively. "I *will* have to see your skills. But I suppose one problem at a time. Right now, I'm just too upset about these roses. I specifically told my gardener I wanted fuchsia roses." He tsked his tongue in agitation.

I walked forward, looking critically at the flowers. "Well, you know, BS...." Stephon flicked a critical glance in my direction. "The problem is, your average male"—I pointedly looked at Andrew, who rolled his eyes—"can only see the sixteen basic colors. They just don't see the difference between hot pink and fuchsia, or mint green and sea foam."

"You know, I think you're right, LB. But the gardener does such a wonderful job otherwise." He motioned to the impeccable grass and the vine-covered arbors. The yard was spectacular.

"It's just not a gift God has granted him," I said. "Now, every once in a while a more gifted man, such as yourself, will come along and have the discernment to know the difference, but it can be such a burden when others don't have the same gifts." I crossed an arm over my chest, rested the elbow of my other arm on my wrist, and tapped my chin as if deep in thought. "You know, you might consider sending Victoria with your gardener when he goes to pick out new plants. I'm sure she'd be more than capable of getting the right color, while the gardener can continue to choose the healthy plants." With one stroke I'd gotten even with the snotty Victoria and her dismissive attitude. Thinking of Victoria stumbling through greenhouses in her stilettos, surrounded by fertilizer, made me smile.

"Now, that really is an excellent idea. Victoria does have such discerning taste; I'm sure you're right." Stephon grinned absently as he looked at the flowers. Charlie snorted and tittered behind the rest of the guard.

Andrew stepped forward to stand at my side, looking surprised. He couldn't believe my outrageous behavior. Even if I wasn't a high-maintenance man, that didn't mean I couldn't appreciate someone being themselves. Stephon had lived a long life, and if he chose to be flamboyant, more power to the man.

When in Rome, my love. Now be nice and let me handle Stephon; we're making friends. If it takes a bit of dramatic behavior, I can do that. I did odder things to get along in new families when I was a foster kid, I told Andrew, my tone clearly amused.

Stephon continued to address me as LB, or little bitch, every chance he got, while I continued to insult him by calling him blood sucker or BS, but at the same time, we seemed to be getting along much better than I think either of us expected. I could tell Andrew felt at a complete loss for words, a little upset he kept getting blamed for things he wasn't really sure were his fault. I kissed him in my mind. *I love you and I'll explain it all later. Try not to distract me. I really need to focus to keep up with him.*

Fine, but I really don't get what you're doing, Andrew grumbled.

"You know, LB, we really do need to talk. I mean, this whole business about your parents is hard to swallow. And to have been raised by humans—of all the horrible things to go through. You're simply going to have to tell me everything." Stephon put an arm around my waist, and I draped mine about him. I let him lead me out of the garden area and toward the front steps of the house as if we were old friends.

"It really is quite the story… I still shudder when I think of the past. It's still painful and some wounds take a while to heal. You understand." Thoughts of my past had my act slipping a bit, but I knew he needed to hear the bad along with the good. I didn't intend to give him a lot of the details of my youth, but he needed to know the basics, especially if he was to be an ally.

"Come along, Poodle, don't dawdle… and bring your friends. There's room for everyone," Stephon called back to Andrew, who stood still, a bit stunned. Tim came up behind him as we started moving off and put a reassuring hand on Andrew's shoulder. Charlie kept pace with me and Stephon as she continually tried to stifle her snickers. If she couldn't get a grip, I'd make her stay outside. She was just being rude. Things were going pretty well at the moment, and I wanted them to stay that way. Yes, admittedly, I was not behaving as I usually do, and eventually I'd have to be more myself. This was about what Stephon needed to help him get over my mate—that preferably wouldn't end in me killing him—and I didn't need Charlie ruining it. If Stephon needed a verbal cat fight to prevent a physical all-out claws and fangs clash, I was all for it.

When we got into the house, Victoria stood at the door with a clipboard and a pen, as though she had a schedule for Stephon that needed to be adhered to, although I couldn't imagine what kind of schedule he needed up here on a mountainside. Her two guards stood behind her, looking impressive, which I knew had to be their job more than anything else.

"Victoria, be a dear and cancel all my appointments for today. And the next couple of days. LB and Poodle are going to be taking up most of my time. Oh, and I have another errand for you. I need you to go with the gardener. The roses he chose are *not* the right color. He got hot pink and I need fuchsia. Can you please make sure he gets the right color this time? Thank you, love, you're such a dear." Stephon dismissed her and the guards with a wave of his hand, sending them from the room. Victoria looked at me, enraged. I smiled sweetly at her, my arm still around Stephon's waist and his around mine. Andrew, Tim, and Charlie followed along behind us, leaving the rest of the guard scattered around the area. Of course Victoria had no idea I'd suggested she assist the gardener, but it still felt good. Charlie had finally gotten a hold of her giggles as she watched the guards leave the room.

Stephon showed us through the porch and into the main house. Everything about the house seemed light and impeccably decorated. There wasn't one item or corner overlooked. We went into a small sitting room. It was cozy and warm, a comfortable, intimate nook.

"Poodle, love, please find something relaxing on the stereo. You know what I like." Stephon waved his hand at Andrew. The man couldn't help it—he talked with his hands as much as his words. Andrew went to the corner of the room and began fiddling with some dials on the wall. The house had been wired for sound. "Please, sit down, be comfortable," Stephon said to Tim and Charlie, who hovered by the door. Stephon then turned to me. Holding me at a slight distance, he looked at me with a critical eye. "I'm guessing a 30 regular." He scrutinized my hips, nodding to himself.

"Yes indeed." I grinned, amazed he could discern my size just by looking.

"Thought so. Linda… Grace…," Stephon called, though he barely raised his voice.

Two vampires dressed in maids' uniforms appeared at the door.

"My Poodle did LB a disservice, and I mean to rectify it. He is a small, 30 regular, and will need something from the Klein collection, I think. A nice tailored pant, a two-button sweater in browns, and a tan T-shirt should do nicely. But first, please bring me a large bathroom towel." Stephon let me go then, and I gave him a warm smile as soft jazz began to play on the overhead system. Andrew came up behind me and put his hands on my shoulders. He pulled me back against his chest. Andrew was feeling very possessive of me, and having Stephon walk between us, with an arm around my waist, had been difficult for him to tolerate. Stephon turned, removed his apron, and handed it to the maid who'd remained, then draped himself over one of the chairs.

Are you okay? Andrew growled softly, placing a possessive kiss upon my neck. I turned and cupped his cheek, reassuring him with my touch and my thoughts.

"I'm good, love. Can you please help me with the towel like we did before?" *I'll do the falcon first, then go through the others. So after I become the falcon, you'll need to step back, okay? I'll finish with the falcon again.* Andrew nodded his understanding. Stephon seemed lost in the music and unaware of our conversation. One of the maids reappeared with the towel.

"This way, sir." She led me through the door in the sitting room to an attached room. Charlie followed closely, leaving Tim with Andrew and Stephon. I walked into a bathroom, and the maid handed the towel to Charlie and excused herself, closing the door behind her.

"You could've told me he had the hots for Andrew!" I hissed at Charlie softly.

"I had no idea. I've never met him before, and Tim never said anything." Charlie snickered. "If I'd known, trust me, I would've told you. You realize he's probably been crushing on Andrew for years, maybe even decades."

"I know, and you aren't helping by reminding me! Andrew, on the other hand, is completely oblivious and denies it, even now that I've shown him. He just can't wrap his mind around Stephon being in love with him. I'm sure the more females Andrew refused, the more sure Stephon became that my mate would eventually realize he cared about him and the two of them could be happy together." I groaned as I pulled my shirt over my head and handed it to Charlie. "Now it's not going to happen, and I can hardly imagine waiting years for someone to love me only to have him snatched away."

Andrew's irritated growl flowed through our connection. *You are the only one I want. Even if Stephon does have a crush, I couldn't return those feelings any more than I could to the women he wanted me to choose from.*

Be calm, love, I thought to him. *Stephon's watching you for any unusual behavior. I know you love me.* Charlie turned her back to me as I dropped my pants and wrapped the towel about my hips. I picked up my clothes, folded them, and placed them on the bathroom counter. "Come on, let's get this over with." Charlie turned around, and upon seeing me clad in the towel, opened the door and led the way back into the sitting room. Andrew stood as we entered the room. The calm mask placed tightly over his emotions hid Andrew's frustration, but his eyes still lit up when I walked into the room. He instantly claimed me and pulled me against him, then crossed his arms in front of my chest as we faced Stephon.

Sighing at once again feeling like a sideshow act at a carnival, I dropped all pretense of playing games. I didn't want Stephon to think I wasn't serious. "I have a few selections for you. I want there to be no mistake—" I paused as I met Stephon's violet gaze. I didn't blink as his silent challenge flashed warningly. But it was a toothless threat. There was nothing he could do to me that wouldn't hurt Andrew, and Stephon wouldn't willingly cause my mate pain. "Everything I do, Andrew can do as well." I let the love in my voice show as I turned from Stephon to look up into Andrew's eyes for a moment.

Returning to Stephon, I couldn't help but notice a look of sour grapes on his face. I knew he could see the love we had for one another. I felt bad for him, but soon he'd have more to think about than his unrequited love. With a smile, I opened my eyes a little wider and let the power of my wolf show very clearly. Stephon paled, and I couldn't help but be amazed; I didn't think a vampire could get any more washed out. It was clear he saw the animal in my eyes. I let go of the towel, knowing Andrew held it, and opened my arms wide, letting the quicksilver take me.

The black falcon was first onstage. I purposely slowed the transformation so Andrew could move with me, keeping my dignity covered with the towel, until I was wrapped in my feathers. *Kak kak kak*, I called, and Andrew drew back, tightly wrapping the towel around his arm to protect it from my talons. With a single flap of my wings, I took a perch on the towel. Andrew carried me over so Stephon could inspect me closely and also to prove I could hold the shape for as long as I wanted to. I spread my wings, allowing Stephon a better look at the red-tipped flight feathers and the black plumage on my chest.

"Magnificent. He's a very beautiful falcon," Stephon remarked, sounding somewhat impressed.

"You ain't seen nothin' yet." Andrew stroked his hand along my back, caressing my feathers, before he stepped back, letting me flutter to the ground.

Once Andrew had moved away, I let the change happen. The quicksilver washed over my feathered body, replacing it with the chocolate-brown wolf. Stephon's eyes practically bugged out as he watched me go from one animal form to another. I pranced about, brushing my tail against his legs, letting him get a good look. The wolf howled, and I noticed Andrew struggling to restrain his accompanying howl. Inwardly, I chuckled while the wolf growled softly at him.

"But he can't do that. He shouldn't be able to do that!" Stephon hollered after picking his jaw up off the floor.

"Watch. He's not done yet," Andrew boasted. I moved from the chocolate wolf into the polar bear.

Thankfully Stephon had cathedral ceilings or my bear would've been decidedly uncomfortable. As I stood up on my hind legs, my head still came uncomfortably close to his chandelier. I snarled, displaying a set of teeth any carnivore would envy before dropping back down on all fours. *You were right, Andrew, an elephant would've been impossible to demonstrate under these conditions.*

Andrew's pride bolstered my mood and even though these demonstrations of my abilities made me feel ridiculous, his amazement and wonder made me feel like less of a freak on display. The quicksilver took me once more, and the bear blurred as I became a Siberian tiger. Without a doubt, my tiger was a showstopper. The black stripes, vivid against my snow-white pelt, were beautifully exotic, and the fangs peeking out from under large lips were deadly serious. My roar shook the windows as I clicked my long claws on the hardwood. The tiger, like the polar bear, had difficulty with the size of the room. I could barely turn around. My tail brushed against Stephon as I turned. Every inhale and exhale was accompanied by a low growl, sending low level vibrations through the room. They'd sat back from the bear, but they physically cringed away from the tiger—all except Andrew. He moved forward and put his arms around my gigantic head and stroked my face.

I didn't get to touch your tiger. Things were so rushed, I didn't realize how majestic you are. My purr caused the crystals in the chandelier to tinkle merrily and I chuffed softly at Andrew. I rubbed my head against him. Then he stood back, knowing the tiger was my last animal before I returned to falcon and, finally, human. The tiger folded back into the falcon, I hopped up onto

Andrew's arm, and we moved back to the center of the room. He held me close, reassuring me. When he held me out a bit from himself, I opened my wings so I could balance and not dig my talons into his arm.

"Wow," Stephon mumbled. "I know you told me, but I couldn't believe.... He really is a pureblood. I haven't seen transformations like those in centuries. Hell, I knew purebloods who couldn't have pulled off those transformations back to back." Stephon looked at Andrew, a shrewd light in his eyes. "You can do just what he did?"

"Yes, and just as easily." Andrew smiled. "Satisfied?"

"Well, yes," Stephon stammered.

I glided to the floor at Andrew's feet. He opened the towel, and I flowed slowly from the falcon back into my human shape again, holding the feathers as long as I could to cover my nudity, though I needn't have been concerned. Andrew moved with me, keeping me covered with the towel as I became myself.

"Why the slowdown in transformation when you go from human to animal and back again?" Stephon asked, frowning.

I answered him with a smile. "I slow down the shift on purpose to make sure Andrew can move with me and keep my nudity covered. I didn't grow up with this, so I'm still a bit shy when it comes to running around naked. Unlike him." I blushed with embarrassment.

"I see. How coarse of me." Stephon nodded slightly. "I've never met a shape-shifter concerned about nudity before." He grinned at me. The two maids appeared out of nowhere and stood waiting in the doorway. "Please, go with Linda and Grace. They'll get you dressed... appropriately." Stephon stood, motioning to the maids to assist. Charlie, who'd guarded the door while I'd put on my demonstration, followed us out of the room.

The two maids led us up a flight of stairs to a large white bedroom with dressing room mirrors and a tailor's pedestal along one wall across from a king-size bed. A chaise lounge sat along one wall, with huge floor-to-ceiling windows covering the outside wall. The shades were drawn, and bright overhead lights illuminated the room. I was shown to the attached bathroom, and while I gawked at the opulence around me, the maids took my towel, baring me for all to see. I protested and they pushed me toward a large antique bathtub filled with hot water. Evidently Stephon felt I needed an immediate spa treatment. They took the leather tie out of my hair and began washing it and me, paying no heed to my protests. Charlie leaned against the open door, watching with amusement.

"Aren't you supposed to be my guard?" I sputtered between dunks under the water to get the soap out of my hair.

She laughed out loud. "No one told me to save you from a bath."

"I'll get even with you one of these days, Charlie," I complained, but it was an empty threat. I couldn't have been fonder of her if she were my sister.

When the maids finally deemed me fully scrubbed, they drained the tub and I climbed out, attempting to cover myself with my hands. They patted me dry, buffing and polishing my skin till it pinked and smarted. They brushed out and dried my hair, then trimmed the ends. They handed me a light-brown pair of pants with tan pinstripes, a tan, deep V-neck T-shirt, and a dark, chocolate-brown cashmere sweater.

My hair hung straight to my shoulders, completely brushed out, smooth as silk. Andrew would be touching it all day. The thought made me smile to myself. I handed the leather tie to Charlie to stash. I'd let my hair hang—at least until it drove me crazy, then Andrew could tie it back for me.

The maids disappeared. Evidently, I was now appropriately dressed to return. Curious about the result of all their fussing, I stood in front of the bathroom mirrors to have a look at myself. I had to admit, I looked *good*. Never in my life had I looked as put together and capable as I did right now. Gone was the delinquent runaway. I hoped Andrew would be pleased. I had to say this for Stephon, the man had an excellent eye for clothing. If he'd dressed up all the girls he'd paraded past Andrew like this, I wasn't surprised Stephon thought he had a chance when Andrew remained unwavering.

"Well, Charlie, what do you think?" I asked, looking at her.

"You look fabulous, Lance. I've never seen you look quite like this. You're dressed to impress and the results are… wow!" Charlie motioned me to go before her as we went out the door and down the stairs.

The men were discussing the merits of my ancient pureblood status as I stood in the doorway, Charlie behind me. When we were noticed, they all rose to their feet.

"Now that is much more like it, darling. See, Poodle, the right cut and color, with a physique like LB's, and next thing you know… royalty. Quite handsome, LB, much more pleasant on the eyes. Now you look like a prince."

Andrew reached out to me, his hands trembling. "You take my breath away." He could barely talk. "I may never let anyone near you again. I want to take you and run as far as I can get." He reached out to touch my hair. In his mind's eye, he compared it to brown silk that flowed around me.

I leaned in and gave him a kiss. "Only for you, my love." I put one hand on his chest and turned him around, back into the room, where Stephon and Tim waited for us. He held my hand, drawing me with him, and I gently nudged him toward the love seat, where we could sit together. He usually had me on his left, but I guided him gently to the left side of the love seat then gracefully draped myself onto his right side. He closed his arms around my waist, holding me molded against him. I'd placed myself between him and Stephon. Once we were seated, both Tim and Stephon retook their seats.

"So, what did you think of my little demonstration?" I asked, not quite sure where to begin.

"You're very talented. Tim's shown me the results of the genetic testing. Your bloodlines are definitely impressive. With your particular family history, you're completely without a benefactor of any kind. Neither lines of your family were thought to exist. Andrew's correct in thinking you're a free spirit," Stephon admitted. "The closest person you'd have to a benefactor would be Lord Basil as a sort of… grandfather."

I could sense his resistance to the idea of Lord Basil becoming our benefactor. Because ultimately if I went to Lord Basil, Andrew would become his beneficiary as well. The two of us were a package deal. The loss Stephon had to be feeling pained me as I thought how I'd feel if I were to lose Andrew.

Never going to happen, leannan, he whispered, his thought as gentle as a kiss.

"I'm glad you liked the show. You have exquisite taste, and your home is phenomenally decorated. Who designed it for you or did you do it yourself?" I flattered him.

He brightened immediately. "I, of course, decorated it myself. I did take an idea here and there from other designers, but I wanted to make it my own. I included some pieces I've collected over the years. You know, little touches here and there, the kind of thing that just finishes a space."

"Well, I know where Andrew gets his flair for interior decorating, then. You should see what he's done with our cottage. You taught him well."

"Thank you. I'm glad something rubbed off in all the time I've been dealing with the brute. If the fashion sense didn't come through, at least design and style has percolated through his thick skull." Stephon eyed Andrew, whose attention was completely engrossed in playing with my hair. He seemed lost in his own world, not paying an iota of attention to our conversation, only to me—at least that was how he appeared. I knew he hadn't missed a word either of us said, despite his apparent preoccupation.

"So, what are we to do with you?" Stephon mused to himself. "How do we assign you a benefactor? I mean, you have vassals of your own that are drones."

"Stephon, I won't be owned." The words were cold. I let them sink in. I'd used his proper name, which I hadn't done since we'd arrived. I wanted him to understand this wasn't up for debate and I wasn't fooling around.

"But…." Stephon frowned as though he wanted to argue the point.

"What are you thinking? I'm not a commodity to be handled and sold. With my bloodline, with what the vampires have been doing to my people, with the murder attempts we've already had to subdue, and finally the changes our mating has caused in Andrew… do you think a vampire should—or even could—control me?" I tried not to let my anger at the entire idea get to me. I tried to remind myself that Stephon wasn't yet ready to let go. "There'll be nothing but questions about where I've come from, and with the changes in Andrew, they'll be looking very closely at his breeding and pedigree. They'll be studying your management practices. What do you think they'll do when they see how strong his family has become under your benevolent care?"

"I've done my duty by Andrew's family. And all of my beneficiaries." Stephon's tone was suddenly icy.

145

"I'm not saying you haven't. I'm exceedingly grateful to you for your generous care of Andrew and his family. But when a pureblood comes from one of your beneficiary bloodlines, something most vampires have been trying to prevent for centuries by diluting the stronger families with human mixes, how will your colleagues look at you?"

Stephon's gaze flew to Tim and Charlie. They both returned his look coldly, judging how far he'd let me push him.

"I must say, LB, you're very well informed for someone so new to our world," Stephon hissed, still staring accusingly at Tim.

"I learn quickly when my life is threatened and the people I love are in danger," I replied.

Stephon took a deep breath and sighed. "They won't like it. There'll probably be inquiries into all my beneficiaries. The least they'll do is remove the families from my care. The most would be to put them all to death." Stephon fidgeted, clenching and unclenching his hands. "For myself, the minimum sentence would be exile from vampire society as a traitor. All my holdings, wealth, and drones would be taken from me. The maximum? I'd be executed. The council would view me as a traitor who turned against his own race. Not all of them would look at it that way, but a majority of the born vampires would. Most aren't as old as I am. They don't remember the times when shifters were our equals and our allies. They don't remember the threat of the fair folk." Stephon refocused on me. Clearly he'd been hoping I'd ask him to take me in as my benefactor, and he'd been considering doing so while trying to think of ways to disguise what I was. The thought of Andrew and me exposing our abilities had never occurred to him.

"I'm not threatening you. I've no wish to cause any harm to any of your beneficiaries, many of whom are part of my family through Andrew. You've been kind to them and they speak highly of you. I don't want to see you hurt in this any more than I want them to come to harm." I softened my tone. "My presence is already known by someone in the vampire community. If the secret wasn't already out, I'd probably take you up on the idea of hiding out, but someone already knows and has tried to kill us. Twice. I don't have the luxury of hiding for much longer. The best way I can protect Andrew and my family is by stepping out of the shadows and into the light. I'm sure to attract more negative attention, but some positive things will come about as well. Many shifters will feel they've hope for the first time in centuries." I let the idea of what I sought to do sink in.

Stephon sat with his hands folded in his lap, quiet for the first time since we'd arrived. I watched a myriad of emotions fly across his face as he considered the possibilities and the consequences.

"You're planning on asking for Right to Rule," he whispered, astounded by the realization of our plan.

Andrew's hands froze for a second at the tone in Stephon's voice. Then he went back to playing with my hair distractedly.

Stephon stood and began pacing about the room. I said nothing, just let him pace, working out for himself what our struggle meant. Occasionally, his hands would flutter in agitation, as if he'd touched a particularly hot or painful thought. I waited patiently for him to come to the conclusion I needed, the only viable option I could see. Of course he'd want to delay his involvement, or even disguise it entirely, if possible.

I knew his dilemma, but there wasn't another viable alternative that would produce the outcome he sought. There was no way for me to be in the spotlight with Andrew and for him to maintain that connection and control. If he did, all of his beneficiaries would come under scrutiny and be in danger. There was no way to hide what Andrew had become. All we had to do was transform, and the difference between what we could do and how other shifters struggled was as apparent as the color of a drone's eyes when compared to those of a born vampire like Stephon.

If Andrew were investigated, his pedigree would be discovered. It'd lead back to his family and Stephon. Stephon growled and hissed as he paced back and forth in irritation, finding no way to keep hold of Andrew, not while protecting the rest of his families and keeping himself hidden from scrutiny for as long as possible.

"There's no need for such agitation. Peace, please," I said. "We have a few suggestions we think will make this easier." I stood and pulled out of Andrew's hands. He whined softly, but I walked over to where Stephon paced and placed a hand lightly on his shoulder. He spun and hissed at me, but calmed when I took his hand.

"Come now. Calm down. It won't help to get worked into a tizzy. Stop it." I gently pulled his arm through mine and held up a hand to the others, indicating I wanted them to remain. I led Stephon back through the house. Charlie, of course, completely ignored me, but she stayed a discreet distance behind us. The semblance of privacy was a complete farce; they would all know what was said. Andrew would know everything I said and thought, and he would relay it to Tim. But movement would help ease Stephon's anxiety. I needed his thoughts to flow in one direction, not 'round in circles, so I took him outside.

I patted his hand as we walked while he watched me in disbelief. Few people—shape-shifters or even other vampires—would take a born vampire by the arm in such a familiar way, especially when they were raging as Stephon had been. I refused to show fear. You shouldn't fear your friends, and I needed him to be a friend, an ally. And I was determined to treat him as such.

We walked down the front steps and followed the garden path around to the side, strolling slowly in the waning light.

"BS," I began. I smiled up at him good-naturedly, gently teasing. "The easiest way to do this would be if you freed Andrew."

"But...," Stephon protested.

"Let me finish, please." I kept a firm grip on his hand. "If you free him, the only one who will know his true bloodline, besides us, will be the one who's already attacked us, and their interest isn't in Andrew, it's in me. I'm the target. If he's free, as a mated pair, we can go by my family name and not his. It'd prevent anyone from connecting him to you and putting any of your other beneficiaries in danger—at least not without taking samples and doing genetic testing to see what family he ultimately belongs to."

"I've watched over him for so long. They all mean so much to me. They're my family." Stephon shook his head, unwilling to let go. "You have no idea how you scared me when their minds were suddenly cut off from me. I didn't know if they were all right or if they'd been killed. I didn't mean to hurt them."

"You *want* to protect them—the work you've done. You *need* to keep from being discovered." We continued to walk along the path through his spectacular gardens. He'd created a restful place with his careful selection of flowers and plants. Stephon relaxed noticeably as we walked, the forward movement of the body seemingly propelling the mind.

"You can't hide it forever. Eventually it will come out that he came from one of my beneficiary families," Stephon insisted.

"Yes, you're right—eventually. But if we're careful, not before the Vampire Council is forced to agree to the Right to Rule and whatever stipulations they may add to the equation. By that time, we can claim his blood was changed over time because of his association with me and our being mated." I shrugged. "Which is true, but time had nothing to do with it. He changed from the moment our mating was consummated and probably even before that. Nevertheless, it'd draw some of the attention from you and back onto my bloodline instead of his."

Stephon nodded his agreement. "Yes, that could work. You should look into your mother's family land holdings as well as Lord Nathaniel's. It'd benefit you to move to your own family lands as soon as possible. The longer you stay near Andrew's family and connections are reinforced there, the more assumptions will be made."

"My other vassal, Brad, is checking on my holdings through Lord Nathaniel and his father, Lord Basil. Sandy's checking on the Fenrir side of my family."

Stephon suddenly stopped. "Brad. No. Tell me you didn't contact that weasel?" He stared straight at me, dread in his eyes.

"Yes, I'm sure the other vassal Tim introduced me to was Brad. He said they'd both been with Lord Nathaniel before he was killed." I tried to be calm, but Stephon's distress was not helping.

"Oh, this is bad, very bad indeed. No wonder you've already had attempts on your life." Stephon clutched my arm. "Tim mustn't have... no, he couldn't have realized. He's been outside of vampire society, working with the shape-shifters so much.... Charlie's one thing.... She's a warrior, but Brad? Oh God, he couldn't have made a worse contact." Stephon let go and moved away from me, running his hand through his hair anxiously.

"Why is contacting Brad a bad thing?" I tried to force myself to remain calm, but Stephon's agitation continued to worsen.

"Call Charlie over here. We're going to need her help, and my guards aren't trained for this type of thing." We moved to the gazebo, and I motioned to Charlie.

She came running as we took seats, a questioning look on her face.

"Did Tim bring Brad in on this thing, Charlie?" asked Stephon pointedly.

"Yes, Brad was a political advisor to Lord Nathaniel. As a born vampire and natural son of Lord Basil and Lady Ilianna, he was expected to sit in chambers with the council from time to time. After our lord's death, Lord Basil took all of us drones who'd sworn fealty to his son back into his own coven. He'd created most of us and wouldn't abandon us to find new covens after his son's death," Charlie stated, confusion coloring her tone. "Brad now holds the position of Father's personal assistant. Tim felt we needed someone who could intercede with the council for us, and he believed Brad would be a good choice. He's a drone kinsman and a vassal to Lord Nathaniel, so he owes his allegiance to Lance."

"Oh dear, this is not good. Lance, you want to know who your enemy is? It's Brad." Stephon took my hand in his. "As Lord Nathaniel's political advisor, Brad would've known the most about Nathaniel's property and household. So his father made Brad head of all his estates after his son was killed. Brad has been his representative for centuries and he has a lot of status within the vampire world. I'd say he's achieved about as much as he possibly can, being a drone and not a born vampire. He has large estates that he controls as if he were one born to power. In fact, the estates he controls belong to Lance. If Lance lives, Brad will be relegated to vassal status and all his achievements will be taken from him. The land will be turned over to Lance, a shifter." Stephon now held my hand, trying to calm me.

I'd been betrayed. If I hadn't been so upset about Andrew being mentally tied to Stephon, I might have caught the jerk in his lies. Only now did I remember how his vow—or lack thereof—had seemed different at the time from what Charlie and Tim had said. I'd blown it off. Though I hadn't liked Brad, I'd trusted him because Tim trusted him. My breathing quickened almost to a pant. I didn't take betrayal very well and was well beyond pissed.

"Calm down, Lance. We'll get him," Charlie snarled. I felt Andrew trembling at the edge of my consciousness, and Tim trying to hold him back.

"I can't help you with this. I can give you whatever information I have, but I can't be involved if you're thinking what I suspect you're thinking." Stephon sighed and continued to pat my hand. "I have other families I must consider. I can't bring the attention of the Vampire Council to my charges."

I called to Andrew in my mind. He and Tim came running out the door and straight to the gazebo.

Charlie remained rooted at our sides, but she couldn't seem to stop snarling and hissing. The moment Andrew came into view, I felt the dam of emotions crack. My clawed fingers pierced the skin of my clenched hands as anger threatened to boil over. Andrew put his arms round me, trying to calm me with his presence.

Andrew's touch and scent succeeded in giving me the balm I needed. I grasped hold of the animal inside me and took control of my anger. This wasn't the first time someone had stabbed me in the back, nor was it likely to be the last. I wanted to hunt Brad down and show the weasel just what a pureblood could do to his little drone ass. Andrew's hold on me prevented me from turning wolf and seeking Brad out immediately. I literally trembled with the desire to hunt him down and rip him to shreds for threatening my family and my love. And for what? Money? Status? I would gladly have left him in control as long as we could claim the land as our territory.

"Well, he won't be telling anyone, will he?" Andrew reasoned. "He'll want to keep this a secret for as long as he can. The longer he can claim to be uninvolved, the better off he'll be. If he can kill us, then nothing changes. If we make ourselves known, he can claim ignorance and escape implication."

"I agree. This is a secret he'd do better to keep. I'm sure the assassins he hired have no idea who they were attacking." Stephon seemed to relax a bit as he watched Andrew hold me and stroke my back, my rage slowly easing.

"Better?" Andrew rubbed his cheek against the top of my head.

"Yes. I'm angry, but I think I can keep it together. It wouldn't do to ruin my new outfit when the betrayer isn't even within reach," I hissed angrily.

"There's my love, practical as always." Andrew stroked my hair.

"I'm so sorry, Lance, Andrew. I really had no idea," Tim said. My doctor couldn't have been more appalled that his choice had brought such awful consequences.

"You didn't know, Tim. I can't blame you for doing your best," I reassured my friend.

Charlie still hissed angrily. I began to wonder if there was more to my bodyguard's anger than my obvious betrayal, but there was no way of knowing, and I doubted Charlie would share.

"You'll need to excuse me. I can't know about anything you plan," Stephon said. "You'll need to discuss it on your own. Nothing happens here. Your issues with your vassal will need to take place on *your own* territory." Stephon looked pointedly at Charlie.

I put an arm through Stephon's and left the other in Andrew's grip. "First things first, people." I took a long, steadying breath. "Stephon, what do you say?"

Stephon smiled sadly. "All things considered, your idea is the most viable one, and it will keep Andrew's connection to his family and my other beneficiaries a secret the longest. Exposure from Brad seems unlikely. If you move off the ranch and to the Fenrir lands or to Lord Nathaniel's holdings, it will keep Andrew's bloodlines hidden for a time. Okay, yes. You have my blessing, and I free you from my obligation, Andrew." Stephon frowned. "I'll register Andrew Reed as deceased a few months ago. It won't stand up to scrutiny but may buy us both some time before the Vampire Council discovers you. I can claim it was a clerical error."

"Thank you, Stephon. I never dreamed…," Andrew stammered, close to tears. He sat stunned. He hadn't believed it possible, but Stephon had just freed him. It had been much easier than I'd thought.

"I'd still like to count you both as my friends." Stephon looked first to Andrew and then down at me.

"Yes, Stephon, I'd like that very much. But not as friends, more like"—I looked at Andrew and he nodded—"family. In the coming days, I believe I'm going to need all the support I can get." I smiled up at Stephon, who returned it warmly. "You've taken care of Andrew and the people I love." I'd begun to like this eccentric man. His mind was quick, and he'd ended up having none of the ogreish behavior I'd anticipated.

"Thank you." Stephon leaned forward and drew me to him, hugging me close.

"I'm so grateful. You'll always be family to me," Andrew said as he reached over and gave Stephon the bracing male-bonding hug… three hard thumps on the back before trying to back away. Stephon clung to him, not letting him retreat as he briefly indulged himself in the warmth of Andrew's arms.

Stephon pulled me back into their arms, and we had an awkward, three-way, embarrassing show of affection that I'll never regret or ever want mentioned by anyone for as long as I live. How strange—a born vampire being cuddled by two shape-shifters.

"Okay, lovebirds, now that we've cleared the air, I'm going into the house to make some arrangements. You'll have all the privacy you need. No one will disturb you. Please come in when you're finished. I'd love to spend some more time getting to know you, LB." Stephon grinned as he wiped a nonexistent tear from his eye, then turned and sashayed through the garden in the direction of the house. "So much to do." He could be heard mumbling to himself as he disappeared around the corner.

CHAPTER 10

"THAT self-righteous, disloyal prick! I'm going to kill him, Tim. I'm going to rip his arms and legs off and leave him out in the sun to roast! How dare he betray us like this!" Charlie fumed.

"Be calm, Charlie. Rage isn't going to help us now." Tim put a hand on her shoulder.

"What do we do? I mean… I know what I *want* to do," I said, my words coming out in growling bursts. "I *want* to get him here, rip him to shreds, and then have a bonfire in his name. But the question is, do we have it out with the man? Or do we wait and use him to our advantage to flush out those against us?"

"I think we need to eliminate him," Andrew said. "We can't have him setting traps for us. He's aware of what we intend to do. We don't need him sabotaging our efforts and trying to kill us the further along we get. We need to take the offensive, throw him off guard." Andrew looked first at Charlie then Tim.

"I agree. We need to do something he wouldn't think of. Something… unorthodox." Tim flashed a fanged smile.

"What if I were to go see Lord Nathaniel's father, Lord Basil? How big a chance is there he'd kill me on sight?"

"He loved his son devoutly. I know he met your mother, but I don't know what their relationship was." Tim looked to Charlie.

"I know they saw each other a couple of times. He seemed fond of her. He questioned their relationship, but he was always a very devoted father and denied his son nothing. Truly, Father is more likely to see you as a gift, a piece of his beloved children. You'd be his grandson. I don't think there'd be anything wrong with going to see him, but it might be better if we could get him here. Of course, we don't have any proof Brad is behind the attacks. If we went there, it'd put me within his reach. He might try something, and I could put him out of our misery discreetly and quietly." Charlie's fangs had dropped, and she all but salivated at the idea. I could see how vampires and shifters would make good allies. We both hungered for the hunt. "Of course, if our unexpected appearance pushed him to attack for fear of being usurped of his holdings by Lance... well, then Lord Basil might take care of Brad for us. I'm sure Father wouldn't appreciate Brad's disloyal behavior. Especially since he's been so generous and rewarded Brad for all his years of service."

Andrew rubbed my back. "The problem is not knowing how Lord Basil will react," he said. "If we could get him here for some reason and introduce you to him where we hold the advantage, instead of in his home, I'd feel safer."

"Yes, but we need a reason for him to come. Maybe if Stephon could be persuaded to invite him under some pretext and one of us took the invite personally?" Tim mused, deep in thought.

"Well, you do have a birthday coming up, my love, and Stephon does love to throw a party," Andrew teased, knowing full well I'd abhor being the center of attention at a party. "He's renowned in social circles for his eccentric parties and odd themes. It could be the perfect neutral venue for introductions."

"A party… I don't think—" I started to say before being interrupted.

"It'll be essential that Stephon keep who Lance is a secret from the other partygoers, except Lord Basil, of course. I'll also expect him to allow me to run the security for the evening. Then it should be perfect!" Charlie practically giggled and clapped her hands with excitement like a schoolgirl. "I'm sure if Lord Basil were to receive an invitation to a birthday party for Lance Fenrir Fitz, he would definitely attend. Do you really think Stephon can pull it off? Throw this birthday party and not tell anyone who it's for?"

"Stephon's favorite type of a party is the last-minute formal bash. His usual complement of drone socialites will attend, just because it's one of Stephon's parties and that's the place to be seen." Andrew nodded. "With Stephon throwing the party, there doesn't need to be a reason. They'll just show up."

"I can deliver the invitation personally. Father is the only one who really needs one. As a born vampire, he can't cross into Stephon's territory without an invitation. Drones can come and go because they are no threat to a born vampire and can't actually challenge for territory, but Lord Basil will have to be formally invited. Even then, any act of violence on Stephon's property would have to be approved by Stephon or it would be seen as a challenge." Tim frowned as he turned from Andrew to me. "Once he's here, we'd be able to judge his reaction to you and see if we can count him as ally or an enemy without him being able to attack. I'm leaning toward ally, though." Tim grinned, warming to the idea. "If everything goes smoothly, introductions will be made and Lord Basil will invite you home to your own lands. Then Charlie and I will be there to take care of Brad."

I had never seen Tim look dangerous before. Any doubts I had about him were quickly cast aside by the deadly look on his face. Like Charlie's, Tim's fangs were just as long and, when crossed, would be just as deadly. He'd told the story enough that I should've remembered. Long before Tim had become a doctor, he had been a warrior, battle-hardened in a violent and bloody war.

"So, if I'm understanding the plan, we need to get Stephon to throw a birthday party for Lance and invite Lord Basil." Andrew looked first to Charlie then to Tim for confirmation.

"Yes" Tim said, "and I'll take the invitation to Father myself to make sure he receives it—*and* see that he doesn't bring Brad to the party. I got this mess started, and I need to try and clean it up." Tim hissed under his breath.

"You've done so much more to help me than I could ever have expected, Tim. Stop beating yourself up over this. We all make mistakes. We'll deal with Brad." I didn't want Tim to take any chances with Lord Basil. It was more important that he come back alive if Lord Basil refused. "If he doesn't want to attend the party, well, then we know he won't be helping and we'll come up with a plan B."

"If he doesn't attend, your secret is out to the council." Charlie sighed.

"There's no guarantee it isn't already out. We've spoken to the representative of the royal family. They could've reported my claims to the vampire council even before sending Grey to the cabin to corroborate my identity." I really didn't like thinking about how precariously hidden my existence was. At any minute the cat could be out of the bag, and I wasn't ready. I wasn't sure I'd ever be ready.

"All of this is just smoke screens, to buy time. This allows us to find as many allies as possible and keep my family as distant from the fallout for as long as possible." Andrew squeezed my hand and I turned to look into his calm eyes. "We'll be ready, whenever the time comes, because we'll be together."

I nodded and took a deep breath, settling my nerves. "So let's go back and see if we can persuade Stephon to throw a party…." I moaned inside. After so many years of learning to be insignificant and fade into the background, being the center of any attention at all went against my nature. *I've never had a birthday party. What should I expect from this party?*

"Never…?" Andrew said out loud, startled a bit by my thought. I could feel him searching my childhood memories, looking for birthday celebrations and finding none.

"No," I told him as Tim and Charlie looked at us in frustration. They'd obviously been around us long enough to be able to tell when one or both of us were conversing mentally and found it annoying at times. "Sorry, I was trying to guess what to expect from a birthday party. I've never had one."

"Never?" Charlie also seemed dumbfounded at the thought.

"Nope. Not one. Growing up like I did, I really didn't want one. Drawing attention to myself rarely turned out well. So birthdays, Christmas… holidays in general were never a big deal, just another day to stay under the radar."

"I believe we now have an irresistible reason for Stephon to throw a birthday party. The chance to give you your *first* birthday party… he'll love it. Especially as it's your nineteenth birthday. Believe me, he'll be salivating at the idea." Andrew grinned. "You'll be lucky if he doesn't make you wear a tux…."

I groaned and they all laughed at my expense.

With tentative plans made, we headed back to the house. I could practically see the gears in Charlie's mind turning. She'd begun to smile rather viciously, her fangs glinting in the porch light then fading as we entered the house. If Charlie had her way,

Brad was a dead man walking. Obviously, she didn't deal with betrayal any better than I did.

I plastered a smile on my face as Stephon came to greet us. "I've a mating present for you, LB," Stephon said. "I'm putting a wardrobe together for you. It'll be ready by evening. I'll even teach you how to use it properly myself. You'll look stunning everywhere you go, as you should. One would hardly expect less of a prince such as yourself." I smiled, pretending to fawn over his extravagant gift, as I was meant to, instead of cringing at the title. And it would be an extravagant gift, full of designer labels I'd never heard of and wouldn't recognize, but I'd look fabulous.

DINNER was an interesting affair, the drones drinking warmed blood from black goblets, while Stephon, Andrew, and I enjoyed rare steaks prepared for us by Stephon's chef.

"Let me get this straight." I watched Stephon pick up his utensils, pausing as he prepared to cut into the meat. "Vampires who are born can eat just like the rest of us?"

"Well, not quite like the rest of you. I can eat lightly and enjoy a meal, if I do so sparingly. But I do require blood for my main sustenance," Stephon explained.

"Unfortunately, with our conversion, blood became our only viable option." Tim daintily sipped from his goblet.

The meal and conversation were enlightening as our host related societal rumor and gossip from the Vampire Council. "So, how did you two meet?" Stephon asked, nibbling at the food on his plate, more sampling and tasting than actually eating.

"Lance was borrowing a few things from the barn when I first saw him." Andrew laughed, and I flushed red with embarrassment.

161

"Do tell." Stephon grinned as Andrew recounted how we met, telling him of the cottage he and the twins rebuilt for me from the remains of the miner's cabin.

"Did you really expect to be able to survive the winter there as a human? I mean, as a shifter, sure. You could become your animal and I suppose live in a cave if you truly needed to survive," Stephon said pointedly.

"I didn't have a lot of options. Going back was out of the question, and I was determined to make it. I'd have probably ended up in a homeless shelter if the weather got too bad. Other than that, I have no idea. And I'm beyond happy I'll never have to find out." I winked at Andrew, and he squeezed my thigh under the table.

Love you. I heard his words in my mind and smiled warmly back at him.

Love you too.

"Well, you should have seen this fool while he was here." Stephon rolled his eyes and taunted Andrew. "He just kept saying, 'They aren't him. None of them are anything like him.' How *I* was supposed to know what 'him' he kept referring to, I'll never know. After days of bringing in the loveliest shifters from the strongest families I know, all I'd get were cryptic comments about 'him.'"

"I couldn't help it. I'd left my heart in the meadow and I hadn't quite realized it yet."

"It took me two weeks to get it out of him that there was someone at the farm he'd fallen in love with. 'Course I'd seen the new jewelry, but I hadn't realized the significance of it until one of the girls asked if this was to be a breeding assignment with an already mated male. The man himself hadn't even realized why he was so torn up. Needless to say, I was a bit upset. I couldn't figure out who he could be talking about." Stephon waved a hand about as he spoke. "Finally he tells me, 'I've fallen in love with a lost pup. I can't live without him. He's the only one for me.' I mean, I hadn't heard of anyone being exiled from their family. I wasn't aware of any shifters roaming around unattended. I feared he'd lost his mind."

"Not my mind, just my heart." Andrew gazed into my eyes. "I had no choice. He simply takes my breath away on a regular basis."

"You know, the entire time you were gone, I was a wreck," I told him. "My heart crumbled a little more every day. I didn't realize how much I loved you until you were gone. When you came back, I vowed there'd never be a time we'd be apart again, ever." I smiled into Andrew's sky-blue eyes. They were overflowing with love for me.

"Oh, love. It can be so beautiful." Stephon clasped his hands, genuinely happy for us—finally.

"Not when you've been watching moments like this for the past several weeks. They'll go on like this indefinitely if you don't stop them," Charlie grumbled and rolled her eyes.

Stephon ignored her. "Well, we have so much to celebrate. Love in itself is worth the good cheer. Can I interest anyone in champagne?" Stephon waved one of the waiters over, and he placed clear goblets on the table and then poured bubbling pink champagne for all.

"Stephon, Lance has a birthday coming up this weekend— his nineteenth. And if you can believe it, the man's never in his entire life had a birthday party. Do you think we can do something to fix that?" Andrew playfully grinned at Stephon, and I looked appropriately embarrassed—not hard to manage, since I sincerely was.

"Never?" Stephon looked totally appalled.

"No," I answered, staring at the table. What was it about birthday parties that everyone thought it was tantamount to a sin that I'd never had one?

"I can most certainly fix that. A party! Oh, what a wonderful idea. LB, you'll simply love my parties. Andrew can tell you, I throw the best bash around." Stephon gushed. "But of course this will be a party, but our secret. We will celebrate extravagantly, but covertly, of course." There were endless things to discuss—decorations, live musicians and dancing. I'd been thinking a little cake and a few balloons, though I should've known better—Stephon only did things on a grand scale; nothing simple would do. I was about to protest when Andrew, with a slight shake of his head, reminded me what this was all about. Yes, it was my first birthday party, but it was also a cover. The more people and the more extravagant, the better. The more this would be seen as just another one of Stephon's wild parties. Another event in a season of social events for status-craving drones everywhere.

"You'll just love one of Stephon's parties. They're the best, and only the most influential drones attend." Andrew grinned.

"Well, those who want to be seen, at least." Stephon chuckled.

"Do you think you could possibly make a connection for us with a special invitation?" Andrew looked deeply into my eyes, his warm and full of love, and then forced his eyes away from me to look at Stephon.

"Anything, Poodle," Stephon said softly. I heard his breath catch. I know what those sky-blue eyes did to me—they were impossible to resist.

"Lance would like to meet Lord Basil. He is the closest thing Lance has to a relative and he would be able to tell him about his mother. Do you think you could invite him to the party?" The vampire never had a chance. I realized Stephon would give Andrew the moon if it were within his power.

"But of course. I'll send a personal invitation to him this evening. I'm sure he would be thrilled to meet you, LB. From what I understand, he was very fond of your mother." Stephon's face fell slightly for a moment, but recovered quickly.

"I'd be happy to take the invitation personally, Stephon. I should go and see my father anyway, since I'm in the neighborhood," Tim amicably offered, and our plan was now in place. I felt bad that we'd manipulated and used Stephon's goodwill toward Andrew in order to meet our own needs. I vowed to never let it happen again. He was family and deserved better.

I devoted the rest of the evening to Stephon. Whatever the vampire wanted me to do, I did it. We had fun, celebrating in any fashion he wished. As soon as we finished with our meal, Stephon led Andrew and me up to the suite where I'd been cleaned up earlier, and I let Stephon go on for hours. He showed me my new wardrobe and how to best use it to my advantage. The bed, chaise, and every other available flat surface were soon covered with outfits, accompanied by explanations of the designer label and the function each was appropriate for. It was grueling yet informative. I took Stephon's lessons to heart since, as a prince, I'd be expected to act and have at least a rudimentary knowledge of such things. He had me in and out of more clothes than I cared to ever see again before it was all packed up and he began to plan what I should wear for the party.

"Okay, come on out," Stephon called. He reclined on the chaise while Andrew sat in the armchair next to him. I was becoming disgruntled. This was the third tuxedo he'd had me try on. I tried to remember my earlier decision to do anything the man wanted, but it was becoming harder by the moment. Each tux looked like just another tux to me. So this one had tails and that one had a waistcoat… they were all tuxedos, and surely any one of them would do. I took a deep breath and opened the bathroom door, then stepped out and onto the tailoring platform. It had become my little catwalk, which amused Stephon.

"Oh, now, this one is very nice. I think it complements your body style quite well." Stephon nodded, a sign that maybe he was finally ready to make a decision as to what he wanted me to wear.

"He does look stunning." Andrew had eyes only for me.

Please, love, get the man to decide already. We've been at this wardrobe stuff for hours, I pleaded with Andrew, promising him anything if he could get Stephon to make a decision.

Anything? Mischief filled my mate's mind.

Lover, I am all yours.

"I really like this one the best, Stephon," Andrew commented.

"Really? I thought maybe the gray…. But this does… hmm." Stephon cocked his head to one side then the other. "You know, I think you're right. This one does suit him best."

"You have exquisite taste, Stephon. You truly are a master," Andrew flattered the vampire.

"Oh, stop already, you'll give me a swelled head—even if you are right." Stephon leaned over and patted Andrew on the arm. "Will you look at the time? I'd better get some phone calls made or this will be a very small party, and we can't have that for your first. Get some rest, kids. Tomorrow's going to be a big day." Stephon leaned against the door. "You truly are a surprise, putting up with an old man's whims like this. You've been a good sport."

"You're family, Stephon. Andrew loves you like a brother, and I must admit I'm growing fond of you myself, BS," I teased.

I could see Stephon becoming much more than an ally. Andrew was right—the vampire was family, and despite my best efforts to hate the man, I just couldn't do it. We were friends. I would probably always be LB; a nickname given in passion or pain always sticks, and with a vampire it'd stick for eternity. I'd stolen his love, so I owed the man. I'd have to see if I could find him a suitable male companion, someone who'd complement him as Andrew did me. Stephon deserved happiness of his own... just not with my man.

I watched the door close behind Stephon and sighed in relief. It had been a very long day. A soft growl sounded in my mind as I watched Andrew stalk from the room into the bathroom. *Something you need, my love?* I teased. I knew what Andrew wanted, what he was searching for. Drawers thumped closed and cabinets rattled as he pawed through their contents, finally coming back into the room with a tube of lube in hand, which he tossed up onto the bed.

The day had been hard on both of us. He needed to claim me. Walking around with Stephon on my arm half the day had made Andrew restless. Seeing the longing looks Stephon gave Andrew had made me jealous as well. As much as Andrew needed to claim me, I needed him just as much.

"I need you." Andrew put his hand 'round my waist, unbuttoned the jacket of my tuxedo and carefully took it off. "Can't rush this, he finally decided upon this tux. I'd hate to damage it in my haste and make you play model again... or would I? It was actually fun seeing you all dressed up. You're a real looker, leannan."

"No, we must be careful. Being Stephon's mannequin once was plenty," I bemoaned as I opened the buttons on the waistcoat and slipped it from my shoulders. I handed it to Andrew, and he carefully draped it under the dinner jacket on the hanger so neither piece would be wrinkled. I took off the suspenders and

167

removed my dress pants, which Andrew also hung, along with my dress shirt. With each piece, he watched me undress... for him.

As he began to remove his sweater, I realized I stood in only my underwear and socks. He came toward me as he took off his clothes. "Whatever the maids did to your hair... please do it again. I've never felt anything so silky in my life."

"I'm not sure if it's what they put on it or how they dried it. I'll have to experiment a bit and see if I can recreate it for you." I chuckled. He grabbed hold of my hips and pulled me against him. I turned my head to the side and let my hair rub against his bare chest.

"Oh God, Lance, that feels so good." Andrew panted. He raised his hand to my head and gripped my hair, but didn't pull. He moved with me as I rubbed my hair across his chest. It amazed me that such a simple thing could give him so much pleasure. Andrew's entire body trembled under my touch. I laid my head in the center of his chest, flicking my tongue out to taste his nipple. Then I closed my lips around the hard nub, sucking, biting, and rolling it between my teeth. Andrew slid his hand along my back, then reached down to cup my ass, trailing his fingers into the crease.

"Ah... Lance, you could make me come just by rubbing your hair across my body." Andrew twitched beneath my touch, making me feel like a god. Knowing I made this big man writhe with pleasure was an ego rush I hoped I'd never get used to. I reached over and tweaked his other nipple, then twisted and rolled it as I worked the other with tongue and teeth.

Andrew growled and I knew my teasing was finished. He swept me up into his arms and carried me to the bed. I landed with a bounce on the soft mattress. Andrew grabbed my ankle, slid off the sock, and tossed it to the floor before kissing the arch of my foot and then moving on to the other. He reached up, grasped the elastic band, stripped my underpants down over my hips and legs, and dropped them to the floor. I propped myself up on my elbows, my thighs wantonly spread. My erection twitched against my stomach, precum oozing from the slit, leaving a trail of wetness across my belly with each breath I took.

Andrew's gaze moved over the contours of my body, the heat of his lust like a physical caress smoldering across my skin. He grasped an ankle with each hand, sliding his fingers slowly up my calves as he crawled onto the bed between my legs. He reached my knees and spread me further open. "You're so sexy. Everything about you calls to me. I can't decide if I want to suck you or eat you."

"I'm all yours," I told him. He dipped his head to kiss my inner thigh, first the left then the right, laving his way up to my cock.

"Hold your knees." Andrew pressed them forward as I lay back, grabbing hold of my legs behind my knees, drawing my ass up for him. The position made me feel vulnerable, but I didn't have long to think about it as Andrew's tongue began to bathe my anus.

My body clenched at the feel of his hot tongue tasting, then eating my ass. Andrew pulled me apart so he could get in closer, deeper. "Fuck!" I screamed.

"I intend to, but not just yet, lover." Andrew's warm breath flowed sensually across my wet hole, making me shiver. He licked a path from my hole to my balls, feathering across the perineum, sending delicious waves of pleasure skittering up my spine. He sucked my balls, one at a time into his mouth, as he sank his finger into my depths and rubbed my prostate.

"Andrew!" My hips bucked uncontrollably as he pressed down on the base of my cock, preventing me from coming or moving. He leisurely licked at my balls like they were an all-day sucker, circling his tongue wetly round and round until I thought I'd lose my mind from the sensations that bombarded me.

A second finger, then a third pressed into me. Andrew left a trail of kisses up the side of my shaft, nibbling along the length, then let his teeth rub against the glans. I came unglued, the sensations overwhelming me as I gripped my thighs, rocking my head back and forth. "I can't take much more... A-Andrew, please... I need," I begged. I was going to come, but I wanted it to be with him. I wanted him inside me.

Andrew snarled as he left my cock. I heard the snap of a lid before the blunt hood of his cock nudged my opening. I wanted him so badly. I ached to have him fill me. Even as ramped up as we both were, Andrew held back. I could feel his desire to slam into me, but he was gentle. He pressed in, stretching the guardian muscle to its delicious max, and there he stilled. His gaze locked on mine as he held himself in check, his thighs quivering, waiting for me to adjust.

I rolled my hips up toward him, letting him know I was ready, and he leaned forward, sliding deep inside, while I rocked my hips up to meet his groin. He leaned down and pressed his lips against mine, delving his tongue deep. I could taste myself on him, and the combination drove me wild. As his tongue danced with mine, he swayed his hips from side to side, stretching me, stroking me from the inside as my body clenched and loosened, milking his shaft.

"Lance...," he growled as he drew back till just the head remained, then he drove back in. My back arched to meet his every stroke as we found our rhythm. The slap of flesh and our passion-filled grunts, and the heady smell of sweat and lust filled the room as the speed of our rutting increased. Andrew wrapped a hand around my cock, fisting the head and then stroking the shaft. "Come, mate!" Andrew ordered as he wildly pounded into me, past all semblance of control.

"Andrew!" I screamed as ribbons of white spunk splattered across my abs and up onto Andrew's chest. My channel clenching, I grasped at him as he thrust deeply and his hot seed filled me. A couple of spastic thrusts followed as aftershocks took us. I let my legs go, and he collapsed at my side, his cock sliding from my body.

Mate, Andrew's mind whispered into mine.

My mate, I answered him. He lay still beside me, holding me close against his chest as our breathing slowed.

Be right back, Andrew whispered into my mind, and I slipped into a light doze. Andrew returned with a warm, wet cloth. His ministrations were gentle as he cleaned me up. The slap of a wet cloth striking tile sounded in the bathroom, Andrew having tossed the rag in that general direction before climbing into bed. He drew the sheet over us as I turned into him, fitting my body against his with the ease of familiarity. This was heaven—my head pillowed on his chest, the steady beat of his heart, his scent, his body wrapped about mine… it all lulled me into a deep sleep.

Love you, leannan.

Love you too.

CHAPTER 11

I COULDN'T stop fidgeting. To say I was a nervous wreck didn't even come close to describing how much I wanted to run and hide. Vampires kept coming; they'd been arriving all afternoon. I had no idea who all Stephon invited, but I hadn't imagined my birthday would draw quite this many guests.

Charlie laughed. "They aren't here for you. They're all young drones trying to climb the social ladder. Stephon has a reputation for being impressed by beauty, and they hope to catch his attention. They are too young to even realize the born vamps don't generally attend a soiree like this. Stephon holds them to amuse himself with the young."

"She's right. He's always loved being surrounded by youth. It makes him feel young to play among them. They've never seen a pureblood shifter, and nobody can tell from your appearance alone what you are unless you show yourself." Andrew said.

They were both probably right, except for Lord Basil. Tim had returned exceedingly pleased with himself. Lord Basil, he'd said, was overjoyed he was invited and would be attending. Tim claimed the vampire couldn't wait to meet me and had wanted to come immediately but the formalities of vampire society didn't allow for him to enter into Stephon's territory until invited.

Other than the *formal flash ball* invitation Stephon sent to his mass of party drones, no one had received any other invites. Excepting the one Tim had hand delivered to Lord Basil. Possible exposure to the council would be limited to Lord Basil. If he were to turn against us and expose us to the council… well, I wasn't ready for that, but I'd gather what support I could and forge ahead. I just hoped Tim was right and Lord Basil did want to meet me.

They had all been so sure this was a good idea, but I was having second thoughts… no, not second thoughts… I was past them and on to third and fourth thoughts. Stephon had said this would be just a few intimate friends when we'd discussed it. Somehow to Stephon, a few intimate friends at a black-tie affair meant a hundred extravagantly dressed drones. They were beginning to fill the foyer, the music room, and, of course, the ballroom. Yes, Stephon had a ballroom in his home. I never would've guessed it, but that was where I'd be making my grand entrance.

Crap!

He'd dressed me personally, forgoing the suit he'd chosen the night before and putting me instead into a white tuxedo with an emerald-green cravat and a green and white brocade waistcoat. I'd never imagined wearing such clothing. Stephon even had a tailor come to make adjustments to the tux, tailoring it specifically to me.

I put my foot down when Stephon brought out a coronet. It was bejeweled and beautiful, but it looked like a tiara a beauty queen would wear.

"But, LB, it's your birthday. You should wear a crown so everyone knows what the occasion is," Stephon groused, holding the circlet in his hands.

"I'm not wearing a tiara! Stephon, I'm supposed to keep a low profile. How can I do that traipsing around like the Queen of Sheba?" I snarled. "If you want someone in a tiara so badly, then you wear it."

"I would if it were *my* birthday. Why do you think I have such a selection of them?" Stephon huffed and put the tiara back in its silver box. I barely caught the smirk and wink he gave Charlie as she took the silver box and handed him a lustrous green bag.

"Stephon—" I was beginning to whine and I knew it, but I couldn't help it the man was driving me beyond my last frazzled nerve.

"Well, fine, then, you'll have to wear the sash instead." Stephon pulled a long swath of emerald-green silk from a bag and wrapped it from my left shoulder to my right hip, then secured it with a large black garnet and silver pin. He also had me wear diamond cufflinks and white gloves. My hair had been brushed straight till it shone and was tied back by a green silk ribbon at the nape of my neck. When I looked in the mirror, I didn't even recognize myself.

Andrew had dressed in a black tuxedo that Stephon kept for him in case he was visiting while a party was scheduled. Andrew also wore a green cravat and waistcoat, but in a darker moss green, which complimented my emerald green.

"Why isn't Andrew wearing a sash?" I grumbled.

"Of course he's not wearing a sash. It's not his birthday, silly." Stephon shook his head as if such things should be self-explanatory. When I caught Tim's grin in the mirror, I realized what I was missing. They were teasing me, taunting me to get my mind off the room full of drones below.

You can't walk into a room of drones as worked up as you are now, leannan. You'll have every eye on you just because

174

you're nervous. Andrew's thoughts soothed my nerves, and although I was far from calm, it was an improvement. I needed to focus on something else for a while.

Andrew looked incredibly handsome and natural in the formal wear, as if he'd been born to wear a monkey suit. Andrew simply sat back in the same armchair he'd been sitting in the day before and watched as Stephon transformed me into a prince before his eyes. Once Stephon declared me fit for his party, he excused himself to go get ready.

I stood in front of the three-way mirror, wondering where this stranger had come from and where my usual self had disappeared to. Yes, it was me in the glass, but at the same time the apparently confident gentleman in no way resembled the nervous mess I felt on the inside.

I've never seen you look so... handsome. "You're not going," Andrew growled. "I don't dare let you be seen like this. Everyone will want to take you away from me."

"Um…. Okay, but I still have to meet Lord Basil," I agreed readily, wanting nothing more than to avoid the party. I didn't know how to be the man in the mirror, and I felt completely out of place.

"He's going." Charlie leaned against the door and rolled her eyes.

"If Andrew says…," I began.

"Not going!" Andrew grabbed me around my waist and pulled me sharply against him, putting his other hand at the nape of my neck, massaging the corded muscles and drawing me into a deep kiss.

"Aw… I knew if I left, this would happen. Andrew, you're rumpling him. Now let go." Stephon swatted at Andrew who ignored him, growling, while he continued to kiss me until I started laughing.

"He's going!" Charlie hissed. I, of course, wasn't allowed a vote. I'd have happily skipped the party, but Charlie and Stephon wouldn't let Andrew's possessiveness rule the day. I was going to the party. Everything we'd planned hinged on me being there and meeting Lord Basil—and possibly drawing out Brad, *if* he'd followed his father here. I wondered if Cinderella had problems with her fairy godmother like I had with Charlie and Stephon. Of course, Cinderella hadn't planned the demise of her wicked stepmother along with attending the party.

Having seen other birthday parties, I knew a typical celebration did not involve tuxedos and blood in wine goblets, but then a typical birthday party didn't involve the extravagant flamboyance of vampires and concealed shape-shifters either. Regardless, I was supposed to be incognito from the rest of the crowd, and I doubted I could achieve that in a white tux. Only Stephon, Andrew, Tim, Charlie, our few guards and, of course, Lord Basil were actually aware of my birthday, regardless of Stephon's jests to the contrary. To the rest of Stephon's guests, this was just another party, one that Stephon had thrown at the last minute, as was his current style.

"I'm going to see to our guests. You need to make your entrance when Grace comes to get you. Timing is everything at these events, so, please, don't let Andrew rumple you anymore," Stephon whined before heading out to meet and greet.

"Does he really do this all the time?" I shook my head in amazement. Stephon seemed so excited.

"Actually, yes. A few years ago, he decided to throw last-minute parties because regular parties had become dull. So he'd throw a party and give his chosen guests all of maybe twenty-four hours' notice—sometimes just a couple of hours—and see who'd attend and what they'd be wearing. It became quite the rage in vampire society. Several others even took to copying his game."

Andrew chuckled. "He was so angry they'd copied him, he quit having parties for six months."

My nerves were beginning to frazzle. I could hear music and the sound of the people milling around downstairs. Andrew and Charlie kept up a light conversation, trying to keep me calm. It didn't work. I paced along the covered bank of windows, my beast feeling every bit like a caged animal. An hour later a maid, Grace, I think, knocked on the door. "Lord Stephon says to let you know it's time."

After taking a deep, steadying breath, I let Andrew take my arm and lead me to the balcony above the dance floor. The small orchestra played "Happy Birthday," and everyone stood around, singing, "Happy birthday to you, happy birthday to you." I couldn't help myself. I trembled with emotions I hadn't known I possessed. The crowd wasn't looking at me and although they were singing, they didn't know it was for me, but it didn't matter. I knew. I'd always told myself it didn't matter that I didn't have birthdays or Christmas or other holidays, and yet here I was trying not to bawl like a child. If not for Andrew's arm around my waist, I think I'd have fallen apart.

Happy birthday, my love. Andrew's warm thoughts kept me centered even as a storm of emotions threatened to drown me. He took my hand and led me down the stairs. I'd never seen anything like it. The dance floor was filled with colorful couples swirling and twirling gracefully. I'd been worried about standing out, but compared to them we were clearly dressed conservatively. The dancers appeared completely synchronized. If I hadn't known better, I would've sworn they were choreographed, but then again, no one was as naturally graceful as a vampire—except maybe a shape-shifter.

I had no idea how to dance. Andrew, of course, having spent so much time here, did. He wouldn't let me make a fool of myself. I trusted him as he swept me onto the dance floor. At first

I hid my face in his chest, but as I relaxed and let him lead me through the steps, I looked around and saw we weren't the only male couple on the dance floor.

If you must be nervous about something, then be nervous about us being the only shape-shifters at this party. Nobody will care that we're both male. "Tonight, my love, you truly are a prince," Andrew whispered. A pause in the music allowed us to retreat from the dance floor in search of refreshments.

My entrance had accomplished two things: Lord Basil would recognize me and know who I was, and it heralded my first birthday party. Andrew and I wandered about the party with Tim and Charlie in tow. They were my escorts and would ensure my introduction to Lord Basil.

Stephon had outdone himself. There were flowers everywhere, and music flowed through every room of the house. He'd given me a fairy-tale ball, just like in the movies. I'd never imagined something like this could actually take place. The best part was I didn't have to look for my Prince Charming—he held my hand and never let me go.

"Have I told you tonight how completely and devastatingly handsome you look?" I leaned in, pretending to whisper something in his ear, but kissed his neck instead.

"No fair. We're supposed to be respectable. Stephon won't forgive necking at his party, regardless of whether you're the birthday boy." Andrew sneaked his hand under my coat and pinched my ass.

I watched as Tim stepped forward to greet another vampire. The man seemed uncomfortable and stood out a bit from the rest. He appeared aloof, even amongst his own people. He was dressed quite dashingly in a dark-gray tuxedo, masterfully tailored. He had a cloak draped about his shoulders that hung to just below his knees. The style appeared a bit old-fashioned in comparison with what everyone else wore. Andrew was the only person, in my eyes, who looked as elegant. Stephon, even though he was dressed in the height of modern fashion, seemed almost gaudy in comparison to the other guest's dignified refinement. Tim guided the man over to me. I held my head high while keeping a death grip on Andrew's arm. He flinched slightly, and I quickly loosened my grasp. I needed to get ahold of myself before panic set in. I took a deep breath and forced myself to relax.

Calm, love, Andrew whispered in my mind.

"Lance, Andrew, this is Charlie's and my father, Lord Basil. Father, this is Marcus Lance Fenrir Fitz, and his mate, Andrew Fitz." Tim smiled encouragingly at me, his eyes lit up like Christmas. Pride practically flowed from him in waves. Charlie stood back, appearing more relaxed than normal, her father's presence putting her at ease.

I scrutinized him closely. He appeared to be in his forties, with brown hair, neatly cut and combed. His eyes startled me; they were a very vivid emerald green. I almost groaned out loud upon realizing Stephon had dressed me in the color of the man's eyes. My shyness kicked in full blast. I looked down at the floor, the desire to hide suddenly overwhelming. I flushed, feeling faint and claustrophobic with everyone crowding around us.

"Lord Basil, it's so nice to meet you." I held out a trembling hand to shake his.

"Oh, child, that won't do at all. You must call me Grandfather. I loved your mother like a daughter. I won't stand on pretense amongst family. You have no idea how happy I was to receive your invitation." He gently took my hand and then eased me forward into a very light hug. "You look very much like her. But there is some of Henry in you too. Tim told me some of your... trials. I wish I had known of you sooner." Lord Basil spoke softly, as if aware of my need to run. "Is there someplace a bit more private where we can talk?"

"I'm sure we can find a quiet corner… Grandfather." I glanced up to meet his emerald eyes. I couldn't have been more grateful he wanted to get away from the party. Andrew asked Tim, who nodded and looked to Charlie. Charlie took Tim's arm and discreetly led the way out the door and through the gardens to the gazebo. Stephon had even decorated out here. The hundreds of twinkling fairy lights that adorned the gazebo cast a soft glow over everything. It felt magical and much more private than anywhere inside Stephon's home at the moment.

My grandfather looked at me critically, then took off his cloak and draped it around my shoulders. No warmth emanated from the cloak, since his body wasn't warm like my own, but it would warm quickly and keep off the brisk mountain air. He took a seat in the gazebo and guided me to his side. Andrew sat at my other side. He hadn't spoken to my grandfather yet, and I could tell he wanted me to have this moment.

To Andrew, this man, this vampire, was my missing family, one of the people he'd been searching for since the first day we'd met. I, of course, harbored a reticence to trust anyone, as always. But something about this man, with his great dignity and vivid green eyes, spoke to me just as clearly as Andrew's blue eyes. I wanted to trust him, to believe.

"You really are here. I'd always wondered if one day Sasha and Henry would have children. I looked for them through the years, watching for any sign. I hoped the two of them would find a little happiness in their grief. I always believed Sasha would bring her child to me to raise. That she would feel safe and know I'd never turn her away."

"You did?" I could hardly believe my ears. He'd wanted me… looked for me. Well, not me in particular, but Sasha's child.

"Yes. When I found out you'd been born in Denver, my home territory, I could not believe I'd failed you so abysmally. I'm so sorry I didn't rescue you. Sasha brought you practically to my doorstep, and I failed to notice." Grandfather hung his head. "I cannot apologize enough for what you've had to survive. Tim told me about the circumstances of your youth. I would so have preferred you grow up in my household, surrounded by the love you deserved, and the education I could have given you." Lord Basil clearly felt his failure deeply. He hadn't been there for me, but he'd wanted to be. That alone melted some of the fear that surrounded my heart like a glacier.

"Grandfather, please, it's okay, really. If things hadn't gone as they did, I wouldn't have met my very wonderful and loving mate, Andrew." I paused, realizing it was true. I'd come to appreciate that even though my past was painful, it made me who I was, and Andrew loved me just the way I was. "I wouldn't give him up for anything. I wouldn't be the person I am today had things been different." I took his hand shyly and smiled. "I regret nothing, not the awkwardness of my youth, not the fear, not even the pain. It's more than a fair trade to have Andrew for my eternity."

"You're very forgiving, more so than I deserve. I *will* make it up to you. Your territory awaits you. My children and your vassals have kept it in good order, waiting for your arrival. It belongs to you now, you and your mate." Lord Basil smiled, nodding to Andrew. "I would give you the world if I could, child." He patted my hand and sighed.

Now came the difficult part. "Grandfather, we need to talk. I've become part of something bigger for my people, and there are those who want to kill me." I paused, making sure he understood what I was telling him. "By accepting Andrew and me, you're opening yourself up to a lot of trouble. Are you sure you want to be a part of this? I wouldn't blame you if you chose not to become involved. There's much my family, the Fenrirs, have to atone for. So much damage we've caused both races," I

181

whispered, the enormity of the task momentarily overwhelming me.

"You've done nothing of the sort," Grandfather insisted vehemently.

"My Lord, I've tried telling him he's not responsible for what happened long before he was born, but as you can see, it doesn't work." Andrew rolled his eyes. He hated it when I blamed myself.

"My son, please. I'm as much your grandfather as his. Your love for him binds you to me as much as his mother's love for my son binds me to him." Grandfather reached behind me and gripped Andrew's shoulder firmly.

"Thank you, Grandfather." Andrew's tone held nothing but respect for the man. Andrew liked him. I didn't understand why, but Grandfather instantly instilled trust in those around him.

"He comes by that naturally. His mother could be a very stubborn woman. Very determined. Once she got an idea into her head, it became almost impossible to change her mind." Grandfather chuckled. "The current state of your race and the distance their love for my son has put between our races would make her sick, when all she wanted... all *they* wanted was to be closer to him."

"They?" I asked, frowning slightly.

"Yes. Henry and Sasha loved my son as well as each other. Although I know some of the story, only they know everything that happened. The three of them were so in love, and they wanted the world to know and accept them." Grandfather patted my hand reassuringly.

"They were a ménage?" Andrew asked as I struggled to get past my shock.

"Yes, though their relationship had very little to do with the current state of things. Everything was handled inappropriately.

All three families were well known in society and should have been able to get together and resolve peacefully, privately, the issues the three of them mating would have caused. Instead it became blown out of proportion by anger and greed. Once the discord started, men on both sides, who sought to profit from the pain of others, exploited and enflamed the anger with accusations and hatred."

"So my mother being in love with a vampire didn't start a war?" I hesitated to hope.

"No, child. Greed, fear, and hatred started the war." Grandfather patted my knee reassuringly. "Many who grew up as I did, immersed in both the world of shape-shifters and vampires, who fought in the Blood Wars alongside shape-shifters, are no more. It was a conspiracy; we were outraged that our people were turning against our friends. Many tried to rectify the damage and were murdered for their attempts. There are a few of us still around who will support you. More will come around after being reminded of how closely we're bound to each other—the shape-shifters and vampires. How close we once were and should be again. I'll be there every step of the way, never fear. We shall make this right together."

What do you think? I asked Andrew, not wanting to make any decisions that affected us both without him.

I think it's time to go home with your grandfather. You need to take a chance, and we need to be in a territory of our own. He's offering that and much more. Let him help you.

I nodded, agreeing with Andrew. Tim and Charlie beamed at me, clearly thrilled our meeting was going so well and that their father, my grandfather, had taken up our cause. In the face of everyone's overwhelming pleasure at this outcome, I could hardly object, and to be honest, I didn't want to. I, too, trusted those green eyes.

"Okay, we accept your invitation, Grandfather." I smiled up into the face of the man who already considered himself my family. Me, having a real family of my own. How strange and surreal. Sure, I'd adopted Andrew's parents and siblings when we became mates, and they made me feel like I belonged. But now I had a grandfather of my own, and I hoped to keep him.

"Wonderful! As it is your birthday, would you do me the honor of dancing with an old fool like me? We can hardly spend such a joyous occasion with nothing but such heavy subject matter. You should be enjoying yourself." Grandfather grinned down at me. The man wanted to spoil me rotten. I could see it in his eyes. I might just let him, too—at least for a little while. Nobody had ever wanted to spoil me before, except Andrew.

"I'd love to dance with you, Grandfather, but I promised my next dance to my mate." I smiled and looked lovingly into Andrew's eyes. He'd been waiting patiently to hold me in his arms. The stress was weighing on him and he needed to hold me, claim me even if it was just as we waltzed.

"Of course, but I will hold you to your word. I'm next on your dance card." Grandfather arose and offered his arm to Charlie, who smiled and accepted with grace. "Daughter."

With all the anxiety, I hadn't noticed before—Charlie wasn't wearing her usual black leathers but a beautiful black satin gown that flowed over her curves. Tim followed his father and Charlie. I frowned for a moment as I took Andrew's hand. Would Charlie and Tim now be my aunt and uncle? How frighteningly strange—yet reassuring. What an odd family tree I'd come from.

EPILOGUE

ANDREW and I sat in the gazebo until everyone had gone. My guards were still out there, unobtrusively keeping watch, but allowing us our privacy. This moment seemed like the first we'd had to ourselves in what felt like years.

"I have something for you, my leannan." Andrew reached into the breast pocket of his tuxedo jacket and pulled out a box. "Happy birthday, my love."

I couldn't have been more stunned. When did he get me a birthday gift? He'd taken me completely by surprise despite our mental connection, and he was very proud of himself.

I opened the box. Inside was a beautiful pendant. It hung on a black woven cord of Andrew's hair. He'd painted a portrait of his white wolf on a piece of bone mounted in a silver ring, with a diamond at each of the four corners. A silver claw hung from each diamond on the left and right. A small ornate dream catcher hung from the diamond at the bottom, again woven from his silky black hair.

"It's stunning." I handed it back to him so he could secure it around my neck. The pendant hung perfectly between my collarbones.

Andrew caressed it gently. "You will finally have a piece of me as I carry a piece of you. With this, everyone will know I'm yours and you are mine." He gently pulled the ribbon binding my hair, letting it fall loose. He leaned down and laced his fingers at the nape of my neck, then drew me forward. He gently brushed his lips over mine before pressing tightly, caressing my bottom lip with his tongue. I opened for him and let the taste and scent of my mate energize me and calm my frayed emotions. When he drew back to look into my eyes, his love shone so brightly, it warmed me like the sun on a bright summer day.

"Thank you, my love. You're mine, for our eternity." I leaned against his chest, at peace with the world and the stars above. I slipped the necklace beneath the cravat and the tuxedo shirt to lie pressed against my skin. I truly felt like I belonged to him, just as he belonged to me, under our changing moon.

SUI LYNN is a born and raised Midwestern gal. She loves rock 'n' roll but can get a little bit country too. She has been writing for as long as she can remember and is always found with a book or pencil and paper in hand. She has two Cocker Spaniels who are the comic relief in her life. She loves orange soda, *Doctor Who*, and her computer, all of which she could not function without.

Sui received two M/M Goodreads Romance Group nominations: one for Best Paranormal Story of 2012 and the other for Best Word Created for 2012. She has also been nominated for the Preditors & Editors Reader's Poll in the category of "all other" Novels.

Website: http://suilynn.com/
Blog: http://suidlynn.blogspot.com/
Facebook: https://www.facebook.com/sui.lynn.9
Twitter: http://twitter.com/#!/suidlynn

E-mail: sui.d.lynn@gmail.com

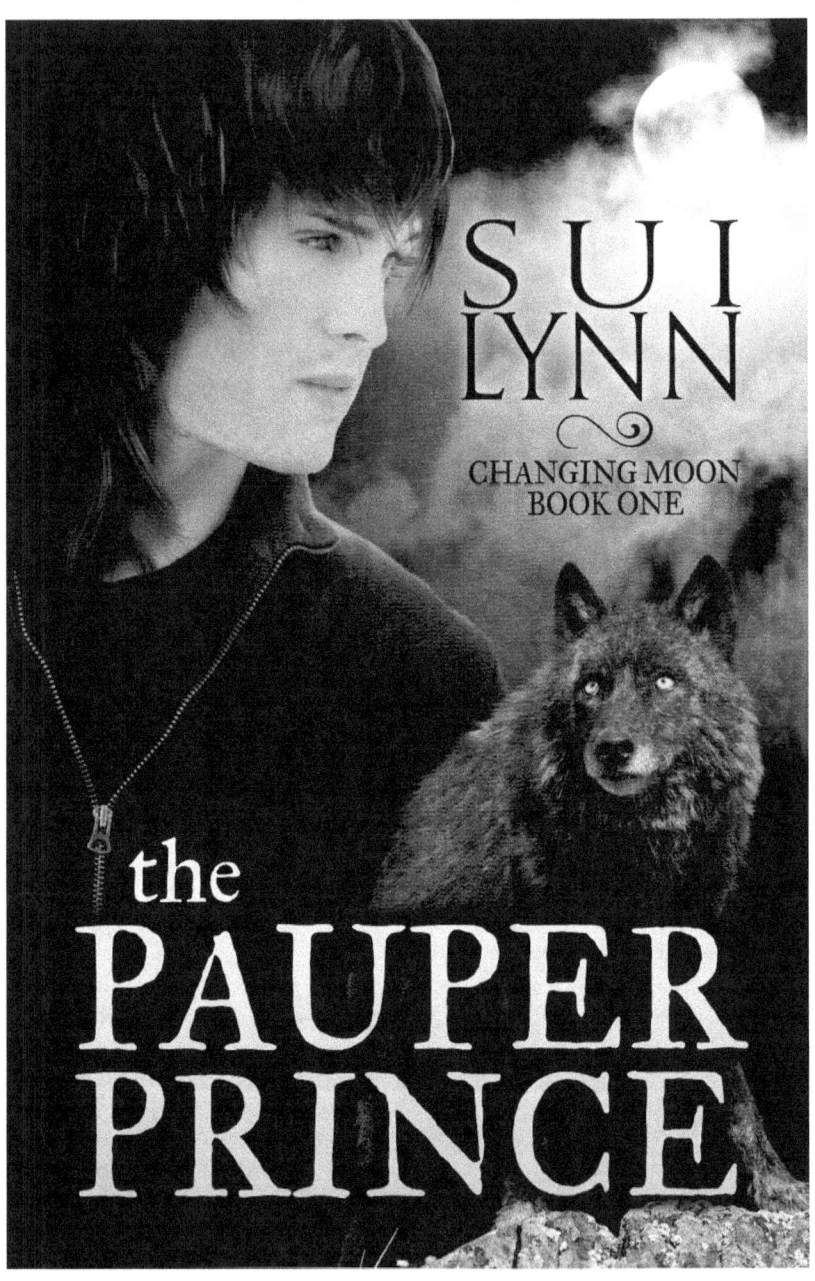

Also by SUI LYNN

http://www.dreamspinnerpress.com

Fantasy Romance from DREAMSPINNER PRESS

Romance from DREAMSPINNER PRESS

http://www.dreamspinnerpress.com